Whose dark or troubled mind will you step into next? Detective or assassin, victim or accomplice? Can you tell reality from delusion, truth from deception, when you're spinning in the whirl of a thriller or trapped in the grip of an unsolvable mystery? You can't trust your senses and you can't trust anyone: you're in the hands of the undisputed masters of crime fiction.

Writers of some of the greatest thrillers and mysteries on earth, who inspired those who followed. Writers whose talents range far and wide—a mathematics genius, a cultural icon, a master of enigma, a legendary dream team. Their books are found on shelves in houses throughout their home countries—from Asia to Europe, and everywhere in between. Timeless books that have been devoured, adored and handed down through the decades. Iconic books that have inspired films, and demand to be read and read again.

So step inside a dizzying world of criminal masterminds with **Pushkin Vertigo**. The only trouble you might have is leaving them behind.

PUSHKIN VERTIGO

Pushkin Vertigo
71–75 Shelton Street
London, WC2H 9JQ

First published in Italian as *L'albergo delle Tre Rose* by Aurora in 1936

Translation © Jill Foulston, 2016

First published by Pushkin Vertigo in 2016

1 3 5 7 9 8 6 4 2

ISBN 978 1 782271 71 0

Text designed and typeset by Tetragon, London
Printed and bound by CPI Group (UK) Ltd, Croydon CR0 4YY

www.pushkinpress.com

1

The rain was coming down in long threads that looked silvery in the glare of the headlamps. A fog, diffuse and smoky, needled the face. An unbroken line of umbrellas bobbed along the pavements. Motor cars in the middle of the road, a few carriages, trams full. At six in the afternoon, Milan was thick with darkness in these first days of December.

Three women darted hurriedly, as if driven by gusts, breaking the lines of pedestrians wherever they could. All three were dressed in black, the fashion at the start of the war, and their little gauze hats were studded with pearls. They wore string half-gloves, and all of them gripped the handles of their umbrellas in the same way, with the bony fingers of their right hands, as if threatening someone with a club. Their profiles were beaked, their eyes bright and alert, and with those chins and noses they seemed to be cleaving the crowd and the heavy mist of fog and rain. How old they were was anyone's guess. Age had fossilized their bodies, and each was so similar to the others that without the colourful hat ribbons under their chins—mauve, claret, black—a person might have thought he was hallucinating, convinced he was seeing the same woman three times in a row.

They climbed up via Ponte Vetero from via dell'Orso, and when they came to the end of the lit pavement they plunged into the shadows of Piazza del Carmine. They instantly breathed a sigh of relief; until then, they'd had to battle through the crowd in single file, and here they found themselves more or less alone, with all the space they needed to trot along towards the church. When they reached the little door the first one pushed it, and they disappeared within.

The man who was following them and who had avoided catching up with them when they were in the piazza now came to a halt in the rain in front of the church. He seemed put out, and stared at the little black door. He passed through the short columns that closed off the porch; the chains were no longer there, only the rings that had once held them. With some difficulty, he unbuttoned his yellow raincoat with one hand and took out his watch. He had to huddle under the glow of the street lamp to see the time. Then he went up to the porch doors and hid there. He closed his umbrella.

He waited, staring at the small church door the whole time. Every now and again a black shadow would cross the piazza and disappear behind the church doors. The fog grew thicker. Half an hour went by, more. The man seemed resigned. He was tall and large, with a smooth, ruddy face under his bowler hat. His eyes were a watery blue-green, his mouth fleshy and sensual. He had propped his umbrella against the wall to dry and was rubbing his hands together with a slow, rhythmic motion which accompanied his interior monologue. He must have reached a conclusion because he suddenly clapped his hands together, as if putting a full stop to a sentence. He turned to look at his watch: 6.38. He grabbed his umbrella, opened it and ran from the porch without once glancing back at the church. It actually seemed as if he was fleeing for fear that the three women in black would come out and see him—the same ones he'd followed there only a short while before.

He entered via Mercato from Piazza del Carmine and then turned into via Pontaccio. Finding himself in front of a huge glass door that led into a vast lobby, all lit up, he opened it and went in. THE HOTEL OF THE THREE ROSES could be read on the glass door in large letters, and behind the glass hung a menu.

Inside the lobby, the man looked like someone who feels at home. He left his umbrella in a large, shiny brass stand near the door, pushed his hat back on his head and went to sit on a wicker sofa in the far corner, under a standard lamp with a large rose-coloured lampshade. He crossed his legs and cordially declared, "Foul weather, Signora Maria. I'll bet the radiators in here are cold."

Maria held court at a desk behind an opaque glass partition that divided the lobby from the dining room and from the corridor leading to the kitchen. She sat there, matronly, already too fat but still hale and hearty, with smooth, firm flesh of a uniform pearly whiteness. She was wearily doodling lines and circles on a piece of paper in front of her, absorbed in some thought—or maybe none. She'd noticed her guest come in and hadn't even bothered to raise her blond head.

"Mario has just gone out to refill the boiler," she said in a hushed, somewhat croaky voice, studiously continuing her doodling.

The man let out a grunt of satisfaction. Then there was silence. All at once he heard a stirring behind the long counter in the dining room.

"Has Mario come back?"

"At your service, Signor Da Como. Here I am."

"An *aperitivo*…"

When he saw the glass in front of him on the wicker table he drank it down in one gulp, clicking his tongue. And then,

9

again, silence. The man drummed his fingers on the table. He stood and went over to warm up by the radiator. Took a few steps, got as far as the stairs and turned back. He hesitated. He put his hands on his stomach, tucking his thumbs into the little pockets of his waistcoat and then stuffing them into his trouser pockets. His hat had fallen back towards his neck even further, to form a sort of halo around his flushed face.

He finally made up his mind and went to lean on his elbows at the manageress's desk. The room was already dark, and only one lamp shone over the front desk. Maria was glued to the counter, where Mario was setting out plates of cold roast, marinated eel and fruit, and also one with prosciutto, salami and mortadella. She barely even seemed to notice him.

"Signora Maria…"

"Mmmm…"

"What time does Signor Virgilio return?"

"The usual time. Why?"

The man went quiet. He put his finger on the white paper, running over the lines and circles as if trying to feel their outlines in relief, for the sake of doing something and to pull himself together. He was embarrassed. He looked up at the woman but his eyes fell to her white neck, its skin so smooth and firm it seemed to lack pores.

"I wanted to ask Virgilio something. But in any case it's the same whether I ask you or him."

"What?"

"I need the usual favour. A hundred lire. I'll pay it back tonight."

"But you already had a hundred the other night. And you're a month behind with the rent. And you have an outstanding bill with Monti for breakfast and lunch that would frighten you. He told me. It's true that it's nothing to do with me. If the waiters want to give credit, that's their business."

"I know. But frighten—frighten who? Not me. I'll pay Monti's bill too. A night goes well, and I settle everything. But I'll pay back the loan of two hundred lire tonight for sure. The Englishman has received money. And he'll play tonight."

Maria's face looked more static than ever. Only her pale lips were somewhat tense. She opened the desk drawer and took out a banknote, her copious bosom moving back as she did so.

"Here's your hundred lire. But it's the last you'll get. I've said the same to your friend Engel. We can't make loans! We're not a bank."

"Thank you. Mario, give me another *aperitivo*."

Just then the glass door opened and the three women in black entered the lobby one after another. Da Como turned to look at them and put his glass down quickly. He smiled and made no hurry to approach them. This time Maria leant over the desk, saw the three women and turned towards the factotum.

"If they'd come five minutes earlier, we'd have saved a hundred lire."

Mario hazarded a smile closer to a grimace. His frog-like mouth lent itself perfectly to that sort of look.

"I really wasn't expecting a visit from you, dear sisters. It makes sense for me to come and see you, but you…"

Da Como spoke with his hands in his pockets. An unlit cigarette, stuck between his lips as soon as he'd seen them, hung from one side of his mouth and his tone was ironic, almost mocking—as it surely wouldn't have been had he stopped them in Piazza del Carmine, when they were going to vespers and he'd lingered in the rain.

"Naturally! Your coming to see us is perfectly understand-able, Carlo. We have a respectable house, we do. And whenever you come, of course, it's always to ask us for something." The first sister, perhaps the eldest of them, spoke. Her claret-coloured hat ribbons trembled under her chin as she uttered those words, though her bloodless lips barely moved.

"And why else should I go there, Adalgisa?"

All four stood near the glass door, the three sisters aligned in front of the man, his hands in his pockets and the cigarette dangling from his lips. Mauve Ribbons shifted, but no sound issued from the mouth of the second sister, who must have been forcibly restraining herself; her eyes were fiery. The last one, however, had a strangely gentle, imploring look, and the corners of her mouth contracted to create two deep furrows, so that she appeared on the verge of tears.

"Carlo," she whispered so softly that her brother could barely hear. He started.

"Well then?"

"We must speak to you," Adalgisa said, as she looked around in disgust.

"Will you sit down?"

"Here?" Mauve Ribbons now spoke and her screechy voice, quivering more in indignation than surprise, rose shrilly above the pitch of the others.

Da Como looked around in turn.

"Yes, here. Where else? You wouldn't want me to take you to my room." He laughed and took the cigarette from his mouth. "Everyone thinks this hotel has only one floor. But there's a little door there, to the right of that landing"—he pointed to the stairs—"and if you open it, you'll see a little stairway like one in a bell-tower. I go to the top to get to my little room…

12

a garret… There are four or five little rooms up there. One for me, one for Engel and the others for the maids and the kitchen boy. It would hardly do for me to receive you in my luxurious apartment, dear sisters."

Adalgisa turned to the other two. Mauve Ribbons pursed her lips, holding back the most biting contempt. Black Ribbons looked ever more imploring, and it was on her that the first sister's eyes fastened.

"It's for Jolanda," she affirmed. "So listen to us, Carlo. We can speak to you just here. Manfredo…"

Da Como smiled, a look of triumph flashing through his eyes. He turned to the imploring sister.

"How is your son, Jolanda?"

She answered quickly. "He's well, Carlo. He's a good boy. He loves you."

"Really? I believe you, even though I've never noticed it. Is that so?"

"Definitely. Manfredo is about to take a wife…"

"Ah!"

"We need to set him up. It's necessary—"

"Naturally! You'd like to give them the Comerio property. Ideal! He could really make something of it. But given that the property is mine… the only thing of mine I haven't already sold… So you're here on an errand."

"Carlo."

"It's not an errand. We're your sisters. The Comerio property has been mortgaged twice. We're doing you a favour to ask, since otherwise you'll be losing it all the same, forced to hand it over to your creditors. We'll pay off the mortgages and we'll offer you…"

Da Como gloated even more. He rocked on his feet, his solid body swaying.

13

"So! You're offering…"

"Five thousand lire."

"Ah!"

"It's a lot. It's too much. But Jolanda wanted to give you as much as possible."

"Dear Jolanda."

"You know, Carlo, Manfredo would so like to have that bit of land."

"Of course, of course! Five thousand! You don't want to sit down, eh?"

"So you accept?"

"No. I refuse. The Comerio property is still mine and I'm keeping it."

The three women started.

"Carlo," Black Ribbons was pleading. But the ribbons on the other two trembled with contained rage.

There was a silence.

"May I offer you a little *grappa*?"

"We're leaving!" Adalgisa commanded and, taking the other two by the arm, she pushed them towards the door.

Da Como hurried to open it.

"Goodbye, dear sisters!"

They were in the middle of the entrance hall and had almost reached the street. They opened their umbrellas.

"You wouldn't have a hundred lire to lend me, would you?"

He laughed, shut the door once more and turned to Maria.

"If you only knew…"

"What?"

"They wanted to give me five thousand lire!"

"And you refused them," scoffed the manageress.

"Exactly. They asked me to sell them the Comerio property."

"Ah! You're serious?"

"Of course."

"And the property is worth more than their offer?"

"No. With two mortgages to pay off, it's worth less. But I refused just to spite them." He paused. "Haven't I ever told you, Signora Maria, that I hate my sisters?" His voice was smooth as he lit his cigarette.

The three women in black walked silently through the rain. The glass door of The Hotel of the Three Roses began to swing on its hinges, back and forth, back and forth, as guests returned for their meals. Maria slowly swivelled round in her chair and switched on the lights in the lobby and the dining room.

2

After nine at night, all the tables in the dining room at The Hotel of the Three Roses were covered with green baize. Once meals had been served, the chief concern of the two waiters was to remove the tablecloths. Bottles of wine and glasses remained on some tables. The guests themselves helped to clear up. Everyone was overcome by a sort of frenzy, and they gambled in there as if it were forced labour. Many remembered and recounted with pleasure how the four most tenacious *scopone* players—Verdulli, Agresti, Pizzoni and Pico—had once sat at the table, cards in hand, nourishing themselves on eggs and cognac for two days and two nights.

And at nine that evening, the 5th of December 1919, Carlo Da Como began to shift around on his bed, where he'd thrown himself completely clothed just after the meeting with his sisters. It was as though the addictive excitement were seeping through the old walls and up to the top floor of the hotel to wake him. He stirred his limbs and, leaning out of bed, felt around for the light switch and flicked it on. A weak, pinkish glow like that of ten electric candles. Just enough, in any case, to reveal the meanness of that room, a garret with rooftop views. A small iron bed, a chest of drawers with a mirror, a washbasin standing on a pedestal, an enamel jug, a couple of chairs. But there was a yellow leather trunk and a suitcase of pigskin. And on the walls, three large colour prints by Vernet.

Authentic ones which, with their galloping horses and flying jockeys, were alone worth everything else illuminated by the dusty lamp. The trunk, the suitcase and three prints were all Da Como had brought back with him from London. Remains of a shipwreck—*his* shipwreck. Apart, of course, from the heavily mortgaged Comerio property.

He smiled. The old girls wanted it to give to Manfredo. Poor Jolanda. Her eyes had pleaded and her voice had whined as she asked him to agree, because it would have been her little boy's greatest joy to possess that property. He'd said no with pleasure. Doing wrong for its own sake made him happy.

He got out of bed and splashed his hands and face with water. He looked at himself in the mirror as he slowly dried off. He wasn't hungry. He would go down now and have Monti give him two prosciutto sandwiches and a glass of beer. If the group were already waiting for him to play piquet, he'd eat while he played.

The group were Engel and Captain Lontario. Every evening, the three of them played piquet from nine until midnight. They kept track of their points in a notebook and at the end of the month they settled up. It was also how Da Como and Engel played when they hadn't a cent in their pockets, and at the month's end, for good or ill, someone took care of it. So there were several months when the captain bore the cost. At 1 a.m., when the piquet, *scopone* and poker were over and the door of the hotel was shut for the night, those who remained got ready for something much more aggressive. They started playing seriously.

Da Como continued studying himself in the mirror. Though he was fifty he hardly looked it; his plump body and his fresh, rosy skin were enough to inspire a young man's envy. But inside he felt tired and worn out. The life he'd led had inevitably taken its toll. Listening closely, he could hear the wheels creaking in his brain and heart. That morning he'd bumped into Doctor Campi, who'd been a student with him in London, and the jolly doctor had cried, "Hello! How's that heart of yours?" But maybe it had been his little joke. Of questionable taste, however, that joke.

He pulled himself together, went to the door and turned off the light—those two switches, one at the entrance, the other beside the bed, were a luxury he'd arranged for himself. He walked into the narrow corridor, which immediately turned a corner. The light from the lamp there, which reached both parts of the corridor, was even weaker than that in his room—and pinker. In that dim light he stopped in front of the closed door to the other little room, which shared a wall with his and opened onto the landing.

"Vilfredo!" he called, and then more quietly, "Engel! Engel!"

When the ensuing silence reassured him that the room was empty, he turned to glance at the other two doors opposite, beyond the stairway, where the kitchen boy and two maids slept. They were closed, of course. He hesitated before going to rap on them. There too: silence. So he turned towards Engel's door, and warily—his every move was stealthy, and he took infinite care to prevent the hinges from squeaking—opened it. He entered the dark room, closing the door behind him. He remained there no more than a few minutes, and when he left a sarcastic smile was creeping over his lips. He started down the stairs, whistling softly.

When he came to the last step before reaching the main staircase—the small stairway that led to the attic rooms joined up with the larger one on one side by way of a small door, which to anyone unaware of the hiding places in that old house seemed only to lead to another room off the first large landing—Da Como took his hand out of his pocket to adjust his tie. Then he stepped onto the brightly lit main staircase and started his descent. The rear part of the building had only one floor, so there were only two flights. From below came the distant hum of the card-players, the sound of bottles and glasses and the audible voices of one or two people in the entrance hall.

Da Como stopped and looked up. A slight woman was coming down from the guest rooms dressed in black and draped with a heavy widow's veil, her golden hair flaming out from beneath a black crêpe hat. Her face was pale, but lit by two enormous eyes with wide blue irises. Her lips were such a bright coral they looked like a gash. Da Como waited for her to go by before resuming his descent, and continued to observe her. The woman did not notice him and moved slowly, looking straight ahead, her face calm and those two bloody lips half open as if in a smile.

"Where the devil has this one come from?" murmured Da Como, and he kept behind her as he descended.

The widow crossed the lobby with the same robotic steps. When she got to the lounge, she spotted an empty table near the arch by the door and went to sit at it. Now she kept her eyes lowered, seemingly unaware of the curiosity she'd aroused. Monti immediately headed towards her, his eyes sparkling more maliciously than ever, his ears keen and straining, an obsequious smile on his lips.

"Is it still possible to eat?"

"But of course. Anything the *signora* desires."

The *signora* nodded yes to everything they offered her, refusing only the wine and asking for mineral water instead.

Monti started for the kitchen, but as he passed the front desk he stopped.

"Room number?"

"Twelve," said Maria.

Monti grabbed a register and quickly consulted it. He read: Mary Alton Vendramini.

"She's foreign?"

"What does it matter to you?"

"Single?"

"Yes. Ooph! What a nosy parker!"

The waiter disappeared down the short corridor towards the kitchen. The card-players immediately went back to work.

"Pass."

"Chip."

"A *terza reale* and three aces," Engel's deep voice announced. He was as large and heavy as an elephant.

Da Como played with a prosciutto sandwich in one hand and his cards in the other.

"It's idiotic to put down your seven in the first round, when you could easily have got rid of your four," Verdulli yelled, his face as red as a cockerel's. The *scopone* table was the loudest. Those four seemed obsessed, and Verdulli—a theatre critic who was by nature always green with bile—seemed keenest. He was actually just the most strident because of his high-pitched voice.

There was already a body in the hotel, and not a single one of the people playing, eating or talking in those rooms knew it. Or at least no one had admitted to knowing anything. So men and women alike reacted with horrified amazement and concern when, at 10.31 precisely, the hunchback Bardi came virtually cartwheeling down the stairs, screaming in his high, cracked voice: "A man has been hanged upstairs! A man has been hanged upstairs!"

He'd actually seen him, poor Bardi. A body dangling from the last level of the stairway that led to the furnished attic rooms, to those garrets from which Da Como had come down not an hour before with that sarcastic smile on his lips. Still yelling, Stefano Bardi crossed the lobby and went into the dining room. As soon as he'd gone past Maria, sitting enthroned under the arch, he had to stop. And he would have fallen had Mario not suddenly leant across the counter and grabbed the lapel of his jacket, pulling him up like a limp puppet. As he did so, the sound of plates loaded with prosciutto and marinated eel could be heard crashing to the floor, shattering at the hunchback's feet.

3

De Vincenzi looked up from the papers in front of him. "Sani!"

"I'm coming," the deputy inspector responded, and straight-away his chair was heard to move.

The inspector went back to his reading: a handwritten sheet of foolscap in clear, well-formed letters such as you'd see in a primary school handwriting exercise. On the sheet was a long list of names. He started to peruse them and then stopped and picked up a smaller piece of paper, typewritten: an unsigned letter, which he slowly reread.

Sani stood waiting in front of his superior's desk. The light from the table lamp—the only one in the head of the flying squad's room—fell from a large green shade in a circle over the papers. The deputy inspector remained in shadow.

"Ah!" De Vincenzi raised his head. "You're here." He showed the letter to Sani. "Have you read it? What do you think?"

"I read it. You left it open on your table."

"You did the right thing." De Vincenzi smiled.

He was younger than his subordinate, but Sani deferred to him with something more than respect. Sani had had him as his immediate superior at the flying squad for only three months, and already he'd learnt to appreciate every one of his merits. Because Carlo De Vincenzi was undoubtedly a man of quality. Rather reserved, and somewhat dreamy, but that faraway air of being absorbed in something hid an exquisite sensitivity and a deep humanity. Sani understood him, and his respect derived chiefly from his friendly devotion, an unforced attachment to him.

"Well? When the chief constable gave it to me this morning, I said to myself somewhat contemptuously: an anonymous letter. But when I read it, I had a strange impression…" He stopped, then added, "It's anonymous, and it was written by a woman."

"How do you know?"

"Every sentence of this letter reveals an unwholesome hysteria which couldn't possibly be a man's. Listen." He read slowly, stopping after every sentence:

> There's a place in Milan where people gamble furiously all night. And that's not all: everyone who frequents the place or lives there is hiding a secret he cannot confess, one that informs all his actions, and leads to terrible things.

He looked up. "No man would have used a phrase like that. Only a woman could have written it. It's obviously nothing but a passage from a romantic novel."

> A gathering of addicts and degenerates live at The Hotel of the Three Roses. A horrible drama is brewing, one that will blow up if the police don't intervene in time. A young girl is about to lose her innocence. Several people's lives are threatened. I cannot tell you more right now. But the devil is grinning from every corner of that house.

"And that's how it ends. There's nothing else, do you see? Just some typing on a half-sheet of paper."

"Is it a joke?"

De Vincenzi shook his head.

"It's not a joke. It cannot be a joke, precisely because it is ridiculous."

"It could have been written by some crazy person."

"*Could* have been, perhaps; but I'm not convinced. I tell you it's my intuition, and nothing else. I wouldn't be at all surprised if something happened in that hotel. So much so that I immediately asked the Garibaldi station to let me have a list of the guests actually staying at The Hotel of the Three Roses. Here it is. I received it a short time ago."

"And what did you find there?"

Sani couldn't conceal his scepticism. It seemed to him for the first time since he'd started working with De Vincenzi that he was wasting his time. How could anyone take a letter like that seriously?

"Their names, of course. What else would there be? Right now they don't say a thing to me, even though the branch inspector, guessing what I might want, added all the information he could find on each individual after his or her name. There are about ten women and around twenty men, including the manager of the hotel, his family and the staff." De Vincenzi now took the sheet of foolscap in his hands and studied it. "In any case, something is strange, and it strikes one right away. Look!" He counted quickly, running his finger down the list. "Five of the guests are from London and have been staying there for a long time. Vilfredo Engel, Carlo Da Como, Nicola Al Righetti—that one's an American of Italian origin—and Carin Nolan, a fairly young Norwegian, not even twenty."

"The threatened innocent," Sani joked.

"Maybe... And another Englishman, also quite young: Douglas Layng. He's twenty-five."

"There's nothing that strange, is there, about five people from abroad running into one another in the same hotel in Milan?"

"Quite. Not if they knew one another beforehand or if the hotel they'd descended on were one of those known to foreigners. But how do you think anyone in London would ever have heard of The Hotel of the Three Roses?"

Sani kept quiet. De Vincenzi's logic wasn't convincing him.

Meanwhile, De Vincenzi continued to scan the list of names. "What an odd assortment of people," he murmured. "And do you know who the last traveller was to arrive in this hotel, just this morning? It's a woman, and she, too, came from London. Signora Mary Alton Vendramini."

"An Italian—"

"—with an English name. She's the widow of Major Alton." The inspector folded the report from his colleague at the Garibaldi station in four. "I wonder why this lady has actually come to such an unknown third-rate hotel, however centrally located it may be—it's certainly not the kind you just stumble upon."

"Someone must have told her about it. Or maybe she knew about it before she went abroad."

De Vincenzi got up. "It could very well be that my so-called intuition is playing a dirty trick on me by getting me to chase after shadows. In any event, it won't hurt me to go and look in on that hotel tonight." He checked his watch. "It's almost eleven…"

"… and you still have to eat."

"You're right! I let Antonietta know I wasn't coming and she poured all her complaints down the phone. Poor old thing! She loves me like a son, and I am rather like her son, actually, since she fed me with her own milk."

He went to the corner and took his overcoat off the rack. Just then the telephone rang. He turned round as Sani picked it up.

"Hello! Yes, he's coming right away. It's the Garibaldi station asking for you."

De Vincenzi put on his coat and went to the phone.

"Good evening, Bianchi… Oh!" He listened carefully, his face intent, eyes shining. "Yes, of course. Ask for the chief constable and report it to him. And let him know that you've told me. I'll go up and take a look."

He put the receiver down and stood still for a few moments, staring at the table. Sani watched him. He'd gathered that it was something extremely serious. De Vincenzi suddenly started as a thought popped into his head. No. It couldn't be.

"De Vincenzi!"

The inspector shook himself and smiled at his companion. "Something's happened rather sooner than I expected."

"What? You're not going to tell me…"

"Yes," said De Vincenzi. "There's a dead man at The Hotel of the Three Roses. And he—he's one of the five we've been talking about."

"No!" Sani protested. "Dead… how did he die?"

"By hanging."

"Suicide?"

"It seems so. But I…" De Vincenzi shook his head vigorously and raised his shoulders. "No. I don't believe anything any more. I don't want to believe anything." He walked around the table, grabbed the report with the list of names and the anonymous letter and put them in his pocket. "I'm going up to see the chief constable. They may give me the case. Don't think I'm asking for it to get ahead… It's not that." He paused.

26

He sounded deeply troubled. "But I have a feeling, I have a feeling—do you understand?—that *the devil is truly grinning from every corner of that house* and it won't be so easy to prevent more deaths." He headed for the door.

"Wait for me, Sani. I'll return and then you'll come with me."

The chief put down the receiver and ran a hand through his shiny hair, which was perfectly parted down the middle of his head. He moved his hand down from his hair to the boutonnière of his jacket to touch the flower: a red flower on a heavy grey suit, perfectly cut. Small, pudgy and very precise in his appearance, he might have seemed anyone other than the chief constable of a big city. But his quick, piercing eyes sometimes gave him away. They were constantly moving, even when they seemed to be laughing in his smooth, rosy face. At that moment, those eyes were sparkling. He reached up to press the buzzer, but a knock at the door stopped him.

"Come in! Oh, it's you. I was ringing in order to alert you, in the hope that you hadn't gone yet."

De Vincenzi bowed, closed the door behind him and walked towards his boss's desk.

"Did you know I'd be calling you?"

"Bianchi told me what's happened at The Hotel of the Three Roses and I thought you'd like to take a look at the anonymous letter that arrived this morning; you sent it on to me."

"Yes." The chief's eyes were laughing now. "But that's not the only reason I called you. I mean for you to take charge of this incident, De Vincenzi." The inspector bowed. "It may be that it's only a suicide…" De Vincenzi shook his head and the chief regarded him for a few minutes. "Maybe. But even if it is a

27

suicide, we'll need to get to the bottom of things. There's gambling in that hotel. The letter may be the product of someone's imagination, or it could be some unthinking person's idiotic joke. But the fact that a man ends up dead there on the evening of the day we receive that letter makes one think. You've been in Milan only three months. Very few people know you. The Hotel of the Three Roses is frequented by literary types, journalists, industrialists, bankers—notable people, as it happens. And by several women... You have no relationships with any of these people. I prefer it that way. You'll have free rein. Are you with me?"

De Vincenzi understood perfectly, including the fact that quite a few of those people were probably known to his chief, who preferred to have someone between himself and them.

"Yes, sir."

"Get in touch with the investigating magistrate regarding urgent procedures, but make sure they let you act on your own for several days. That's easy enough to understand."

"Yes."

"Go on, then. If it wasn't a suicide..." He ran his hand through his hair, touched his flower. "Well, if it wasn't a suicide, you'll let me know tomorrow morning."

De Vincenzi smiled and left. He hurried down the stairs and crossed the courtyard. As soon as he got to his room, where Sani was waiting, he picked up the telephone and called the Porta Garibaldi station. Sani rose from his own desk and went to stand beside him.

"Inspector Bianchi..."

He was told that Bianchi was at The Hotel of the Three Roses. So he grabbed his hat and said, "Come with me. As we go out, tell Cruni to come along."

Not one of the three spoke while waiting on the tram platform. Officer Cruni put a half-cigar in his mouth but didn't dare light it, hoping the inspector would tell him to do so. He had no idea where they were going. Sani looked at De Vincenzi from time to time, but he remained silent and preoccupied.

De Vincenzi himself was profoundly disturbed. He had a vague presentiment that he was about to experience something dreadful.

4

When the three men appeared in the ill-lit entrance of The Hotel of the Three Roses, a tall, sturdy man in a grey hat came from inside the lobby to open the glass door. His overcoat was done up and he had a stick in his right hand. He waited for them.

"Good evening, De Vincenzi."

"Good evening, Bianchi."

Inspector Bianchi shook his colleague's hand and then Sani's; he nodded at Cruni. De Vincenzi entered the lobby; it was deserted. A plainclothes officer stood at the door to the dining room, two others at the bottom of the stairs. Through the dining room windows one could see a few alert faces, eyes shining, and the reflections of a blonde woman's hair. But nothing was stirring in there. Someone, however, was coming downstairs from a long way up, and the sound of their heels rang out on the steps.

De Vincenzi stopped to listen as he looked about. One might have said the entire house shook with those steps. *A heavy man*, he thought, *with all his weight on his heels as he descends. Obese, perhaps.* Why was he so focused on this sound? He noticed a fibre suitcase on the chair in front of the table; a wicker armchair was overturned near the sofa in the large halo of light coming from the pink lampshade. He stood still in the midst of that vast lobby, while Sani and Cruni, perplexed, remained at the door. Bianchi came forward.

"Would you like to see the body?"

"Suicide?"

"No." A sharp negative.

De Vincenzi nodded. How had anyone thought it was suicide? The heels continued to clatter over the floor of the landing and a short, round, obese man appeared at the top of the stairs, just as De Vincenzi had imagined him.

"The doctor," said Bianchi. "He lives just opposite. He's the first one I could find."

The doctor's fat, rosy face still showed his shock, and his bulging eyes were moving every which way as if he were looking for some way out. But he finally stopped in front of De Vincenzi and Bianchi.

"I haven't touched him," he sighed. "It was easy enough to see he was dead. Certainly the first thing to do now is to lay him out on a bed like a good Christian. But I wouldn't have been able to take him down from that rope on my own. The autopsy is tomorrow morning. It's all guesswork without it."

"What are you saying?" De Vincenzi's voice shook with anger. "What if he was still alive? Maybe with artificial respiration..."

The doctor's eyes nearly leapt out of their sockets. "What do you take me for? That man has been dead for at least ten hours and maybe even more. Didn't you know that his dead body is already showing the first signs of secondary flaccidity? The rigor mortis is over."

The athletic Bianchi stared down at the little man. He bent over and took him by the elbows, as if to bring him up to his own level, to look him in the face, as one does with children.

"But Doctor, that man died by hanging! His corpse was actually hanging in the middle of the landing. He must have been hanged only an hour or two ago at the most, or else anyone

31

who went by today or this evening would have seen him. How can you say he's been dead ten hours or more?"

The doctor freed himself and took a step backward. At any other time the situation would have been laughable. He looked like a rubber toy.

"So who are you? Who are you!" he spluttered, practically choking with indignation. "Leave me alone! Didn't you order me to leave my home, come here and climb up to the top floor only to find myself face to face, all on my own, with a corpse? What do you want to know? You're not a doctor!"

De Vincenzi's voice was calm and clear. "Calm down, Doctor. Inspector Bianchi had no intention of offending you. We're here to listen to you—and naturally to accept what you say. But you'll need to explain things to us."

The other man panted furiously for a few more minutes, and then seemed to calm down.

"*He did not die by hanging,*" he uttered slowly and softly, and De Vincenzi felt a quick shiver pass beneath his skin. "*Someone hung him up after he was dead.*"

There was silence.

"Oh!" De Vincenzi finally said. "So, how did he die?"

"I don't know. There's no sign of any wounds, at least obvious ones. He may have been poisoned. We need the autopsy. When they identify the poison, if it was poison, they'll also be able to determine the time of death with greater precision." He rummaged in his pockets and drew out a pair of woollen gloves. He slid them on, pulled up the collar of his overcoat and put on his hat. "I've done my duty… that is, I've done what I can. Now, call the medical officer. Goodnight."

He left quickly, walking between Sani and Cruni, who stood perfectly still, not even offering to open the glass door for him.

He practically ran out, and disappeared immediately into the fog in the streets.

"Come on," said De Vincenzi as he started for the stairs.

"I got here half an hour ago, not even that," said Bianchi. "I had the doctor called and I put everyone I found in the hotel into that room. The doors are being guarded, including the one at the back. I haven't questioned anyone. Two officers are posted on the first-floor corridor to guard the doors to the rooms. There's reason to believe they're empty, because I think all the guests are in there—" and he pointed again to the glass wall of the dining room "—though I can't be sure. There's one more officer upstairs, right up at the top. So it's not true that the doctor was alone with the corpse."

De Vincenzi listened. "Good. You couldn't have done any more, of course. If you want to go, I won't keep you. I'll need you tomorrow, though. Maybe you'll be able to tell me something about—all these people. Something that will help me."

"Uh—" A thought made Bianchi jump. "But didn't you ask me just yesterday for a list of all the guests at the Three Roses?"

"Yes."

"Why did you do that? What a strange coincidence."

"It wasn't a coincidence. I'll tell you why, but not now. It's too soon and… too late. Sani, come with me. Cruni, you stay on guard here. No one must leave, and if someone comes in, keep them here."

Bianchi turned up his coat collar just as the doctor had, thrust his hands in his pockets and left by the door Cruni was holding open for him, waving him off. De Vincenzi climbed the first flight of stairs with Sani following behind him. He went through the small door and then headed up the steep attic stairway. A dusty lamp on every landing gave out a reddish light, only deepening the shadows in the corners and on each flight of stairs. They counted three landings with whitewashed walls, and no doors on any of them, but a window on every landing. De Vincenzi tried looking through the windows. He saw nothing but fog.

They came to the final landing. Right away they saw the black corpse hanging from one of the ceiling beams. A shadow appeared at the door to the left.

"How long have you been here?"

"An eternity, Inspector," said the officer. He wasn't joking. Small and slight as he was, his whole body was shaking, and one could see that it took all his effort to silence the chattering of his teeth.

"Where were you hiding?"

"In there…" and he indicated the corridor, which made a sharp turn. He'd clearly tried to keep out of sight of the hanged man.

De Vincenzi went down the corridor and noticed that the first door was closed, as well as the one at the other end.

"Are these guest rooms?"

"I believe so."

"Did you look to see if they were empty?"

He pushed open the door to the first one: darkness. He went in and lit a match in order to find the light switch, which was next to the bed. The room was empty, but De Vincenzi stood still, staring at the bed. Incredible. Oh! Who was actually living in the room? Sitting on the bed in a gauzy pink dress, her shoulders against the pillow and her pudgy little legs weirdly twisted at the knees was a flaxen-haired doll, her arms reaching out for a hug, her eyes glassy and bright and her chubby cheeks vividly spotted with red. A porcelain doll.

34

"Who lives in this room?"

"I don't know, sir."

Sani came in, pushing the officer aside. He jumped when he saw the doll.

"A woman must live here."

De Vincenzi looked around and pointed to the dresser. On the shelf, perfectly aligned on top of a towel, were a shaving brush, a safety razor, half a dozen blades and a tub of shaving cream. Neither of them said a thing. De Vincenzi looked at the doll again. Sani started to walk around the room. A suitcase was lying open on a small table and he read out the name printed on the card inside the leather tag hanging from the handle: *Vilfredo Engel*. The room at the other end of the corridor was similarly empty; the two inspectors looked at the prints by Vernet.

They found themselves before the hanged man once more. It was awful. That he'd been hanged after his death seemed clear even to someone who knew nothing about medicine: someone had put a rope around his neck without bothering to make a noose. It was his chin that kept him hanging up there. De Vincenzi noted that care had been taken to wind the rope around his ears so that he wouldn't fall out, and the ends of the rope were knotted to an iron rod that stretched from one of the walls on the landing to the other, a hand's breadth from the ceiling. The work could easily have been carried out by a single person, someone who wasn't even that strong. First they'd have knotted the rope, letting it dangle, and then they'd have lifted up the corpse so they could put the head through that wide, makeshift noose. The feet were more than a metre from the floor. So they would have had to climb onto a chair or some such—if not actually a ladder—in order to lift him up.

De Vincenzi looked around. Nothing. He opened the two doors on the right, Mario's room and the two maids' room: empty. In that one, two beds, and in the first room, only one. A few chairs, of course. They could have used any one of those and replaced it later.

They had to take the dead man down now.

"He couldn't have been much more than twenty," Sani murmured.

"Go downstairs and wait for me there," De Vincenzi said to the officer. He turned to Sani. "You go down too, and phone for the emergency medical service to send a doctor and a nurse."

"You're staying up here alone?"

"Send Cruni up here."

Sani practically ran. Halfway down the stairs one could hear him lose his footing and slide down five or six steps.

De Vincenzi slowly turned to look at the hanged man's face. How did he find the strength? He was calm now. The dead man was young, with a fine and delicate profile, a sweet, childish aspect. His open lips showed pure white teeth; he seemed to be smiling.

Why had he been hung up by that rope? Certainly not to make anyone believe he'd hanged himself. Not a soul in the world would have been taken in by it, even for an instant. Or maybe an instant, but only coming upstairs that evening in the dim light and being faced with the corpse. Anyone with a weak heart would have received a dangerous shock. Was that the killer's intention? *To use the dead man to kill someone else?* But how had they managed to get the body all the way up there? And where had it come from? Meanwhile, everyone was downstairs. Actually *everyone*? The four rooms were empty. Surely the frightening spectacle of that body was meant for someone

36

living here in these rooms. But for whom? If one excluded the maids and Mario, there were only two guests left. He heard Cruni's quick, heavy step.

"Oh! Help me get him onto the bed. I'm in here."

The two of them took down the corpse. The empty noose was left dangling from the iron bar.

5

De Vincenzi waited upstairs for the doctor and nurse from the emergency medical service. He stood on the landing, his head just inches from the noose. He stiffened in the silence, willing his nerves not to betray him, not to give in to a sudden collapse. Slowly, methodically, *he tried to take in everything around him*: the light, the imperceptible vibrations emanating from every object, as if absorbing it all by osmosis, through the pores of his skin. The body of Douglas Layng had been hanging for some hours in the very spot he found himself at that moment. From when to when? The killer had been over the same ground. Bianchi had given him the dead man's name when he'd first phoned him, but it had not been mentioned again. Who was Douglas Layng? And how had this young Englishman, apparently rather effeminate and delicate, a Northerner, come to be killed in Italy?

He glanced towards the room where they'd put the body; Cruni seemed to have taken root in front of the open door. Square and stocky, with legs too short for his oversized torso, the sergeant was looking around slowly, cautiously. He wasn't the least disturbed by the body, the silence or the pinkish light casting great whirling shadows in corners, on the stairs and under the archway leading to the corridor. De Vincenzi turned his head away quickly. The sight of his subordinate, the living embodiment of the profession—*his* profession, as it happened—was distracting him from his goal.

The door to Engel's room also remained open, and past the archway, past the empty rectangle of the open door, he could see something glowing in the profound darkness. What light was burning in there? Ah, yes! It had to be the eyes of that doll… But what nonsense. The doll's glass eyes couldn't be glowing! So, what then?

What the devil: the mirror! The mirror hanging over the dresser, reflecting the light from the lamp on the landing. A mirror is always ready to pick up any shimmer from the surrounding environment. Now, he too was *living* in that mirror—and he didn't know it. A mirror was a terrible witness. That one there had spied on him, taken his person too, and reflected his image into the darkness of the room where a rosy doll leant her shoulders against the pillows, her legs twisted at the knees… And in the room at the other end of the corridor, Vernet's thoroughbreds galloped across the wall with simian jockeys in the saddle. Everything continues to live in the dark, even when we think it's all dead. Was the body, then, still living in the dark? In what light was it reflected? A killer! And that horrendous, nightmarish *mise en scène*. It was the first. *Would it be the only one?* A huge, overwhelming sense of danger enveloped De Vincenzi. Someone had written: *the devil is grinning from every corner.* He would have to battle with the devil. Flush him out, give chase.

A voice rose from the bottom of the stairs. Someone was shuffling up the steps. The doctor and nurse. De Vincenzi took out his watch: ten to midnight.

"Doctor, there's a body on the bed in there. The investigating magistrate hasn't been yet. He may not get here till tomorrow. It's rather irregular, but it's crucial that you inform me of the cause of death immediately. I absolutely must have the secrets the body's hiding, which only you and science can get out of it. All of them: how he was killed, how many hours ago... You can take off his clothes. In fact, undress him now and let me have them."

The doctor listened as he stared at the dangling rope. He was a tall man, and so frighteningly thin that he seemed completely shrivelled. He had a long face like a horse's and his skin was taut across his cheeks; his tiny eyes gleamed like topaz. Behind him was the nurse, dressed in a white blouse topped with a cape that had opened up as she'd climbed the stairs. She was rubbing her hands to keep warm. A shock of red hair hung over her forehead.

"Yes," De Vincenzi continued, slowly, and in another tone, trying himself to play down the importance of what he was about to reveal, "he was hu— someone put that noose around his head after his death. Bear that in mind too, Doctor. The rope was wrapped under his chin and behind his ears."

De Vincenzi entered the squalid little room ahead of the doctor and nurse. The doctor stepped over to the bed and put his bony white hand on the body's closed eyelids, on the forehead. He quickly ran his claw-like fingers down to the knees and ankles before moving back up to palpate the stomach. Why the knees and ankles? He lifted a leg, an arm, and let them fall back down. The entire bed jiggled and the iron headboard twice banged against the wall. The doctor turned and took another long look at De Vincenzi—a look of amazement.

"It's not possible to do a thing in this light." And then he said impatiently, "How do you think I can see in here? Can't someone change the lamp?"

"Cruni, go down and get the strongest light you can find. You might take one from the dining room."

"Silvestri, can you give me a hand here? Let's start getting his clothes off."

40

De Vincenzi went out to the landing again. Sani appeared, panting slightly from the climb; De Vincenzi hadn't heard him come up; his footsteps had become confused with Cruni's going down.

"Two foreigners have arrived from the station just now. They've unloaded their trunks and suitcases. They must be English, husband and wife. I had them go into one of the small rooms and asked them to wait there. They didn't complain. They sat down, and the man asked me a couple of times, 'But is this actually The Hotel of the Three Roses?'"

"Elderly?"

"More than elderly. The woman's hair is snowy-white. They're very distinguished; must be rich."

"Go back downstairs. I'll join you shortly." As Sani started down, De Vincenzi shouted out, "And for goodness' sake, don't allow a soul to approach them! They probably don't know."

What had he been thinking? He turned back to the room where the doctor and nurse were getting on with things. He saw the dead man's clothes and underwear heaped on a table. How white and slender his body was! He almost seemed like a child. The doctor was bent over him.

"My word, will you look at this! Someone's stabbed him in the back."

De Vincenzi went over and saw a triangular wound under the shoulder blade where the heart would be, a blackish gash, its edges stiff and purple. There wasn't a drop of blood around it. Someone had definitely cleaned him up. He took the dead man's jacket, his waistcoat and shirt from the table and studied them. No holes. The shirt, too, was free of any traces of blood. Killed in his bed, or else undressed and then dressed again.

"He must have lost a lot of blood."

The doctor replied without turning round. "Perhaps not. If the weapon was left in the wound for a few hours after his death, he'd have bled very little."

Where had the body been kept until it had been brought up here to hang? And how had it been moved, at nine or ten at night, with the hotel full of people and the almost certain risk of bumping into someone—if not on that hidden staircase, then surely along the first-floor corridor, with all its doors to the guest rooms? Or on the large staircase, one flight of which it must definitely have been brought down if it was from one of the first-floor rooms, as it was logical to suppose? Was it possible that Layng had been killed in one of those poky attic rooms and kept there until his killer, or his killers, had thought the moment right to stage this macabre performance? Yes, it was possible. De Vincenzi thought about the long glass wall dividing the lobby from the dining room: so many people in there! He would have to question all of them. Question them? Study them, rather. Analyse them. A feeling of nausea rose in his throat. But he knew that *only the psychological aspects of the crime can reveal the truth.* Well, he'd do what he had to.

Cruni came back with the lamp. "It's the strongest one I could find."

The room, sunk into darkness, was suddenly flooded with a harsh, cold light. The naked body took on clean outlines, as if it had been drawn. The doctor nodded at the nurse, who brought him the little black bag he'd put down on a chair. A very long probe gleamed in his hands and disappeared immediately into the wound.

"The knife pierced the heart."

De Vincenzi was examining the clothes. Nothing in the

42

pockets—not a thing. The jacket bore the name of a London tailor, and was no help at all.

"Doctor, before you go, would you come and speak to me? You'll find me downstairs."

The doctor made an inarticulate sound of assent.

"Cruni, you stay here." De Vincenzi led him to the landing. "No one must touch a thing. If someone comes up, send them back downstairs." He slowly descended the stairs.

Sani was in the lobby. "The two travellers are in there." He pointed to a door at the back of the lobby, past the writing table on the right.

"I'm going in there." But he looked at the glass wall of the dining room. He couldn't see anyone through the glass. What had all those people been doing in there for two hours?

He went into the parlour, where the couple were still sitting. They watched him approach. The woman must once have been beautiful, and she still was for that matter, though her hair was completely white. A real air of distinction, a clear and penetrating gaze. The man was large, his face animated. An enormous diamond sparkled on the small finger of his right hand, which was splayed over his knee. He regarded De Vincenzi silently, responding to his bow with a nod. He then asked in English, "Are you the proprietor? Why have we been asked to come in here? Is this the custom in Italian hotels?"

De Vincenzi had a moment of almost paralysing doubt. What if these two were the dead man's parents? How to give them the news? What would they do?

"I beg your pardon," he replied in English. "I am not the proprietor of this hotel. I am a police inspector."

He saw a look of apprehension flash through the woman's eyes. Her husband furrowed his brow and stood up suddenly.

43

"What do you want with me?" he asked in a sharp voice. "I don't understand!"

What didn't he understand—or what was it he was hastening to confirm that he did not understand?

"A most dreadful event has taken place in this hotel. A man has been found dead, and an inquest has been opened. It will be necessary for you kindly to go to another hotel. It won't be possible for you to have a room here for another few hours."

The woman stood up now as well. "A dead man!" Her eyes were brimming with terror. "But we can't go to another hotel."

"Something dreadful? Ah…" The man sat back down. "We'll wait. We must stay here in this hotel."

De Vincenzi breathed a sigh of relief. No. He'd been mistaken. They couldn't be the parents of young Layng, or else the woman would already have uttered the name of her son.

"Would you mind showing me your passport?"

The man pulled from his pocket a small blue booklet with a large golden coat of arms stamped in the middle: the coat of arms of the United Kingdom of Great Britain and Ireland.

De Vincenzi read the name: George Flemington. "That's fine," he said. "Would you kindly stay here? You may be waiting for some time."

"Could someone at least bring me a bottle of whisky…"

"I'll see to it that they do."

As De Vincenzi started for the door, he heard the wife whisper, "Oh, George! What does all of this mean?"

And then he heard the man's laugh. The sound of that laugh—low, cruel and sarcastic—echoed in his ears long after he'd closed the parlour door to find himself once more in the empty lobby with the fibre suitcase and the overturned armchair.

6

The pendulum clock in the dining room tolled brightly. The new day had begun half an hour ago.

De Vincenzi sat down on the wicker sofa under the rosy lampshade. He found a newspaper on the table and folded it in four. He was holding a short silver pencil, its lead retracted, and he played with it, batting the end against the newspaper. Bianchi had left four officers with him and they were guarding the lobby doors. Sani, in front of the inspector, occasionally turned to observe them.

"Have the hotel owner come here," said De Vincenzi. But he immediately got up again. "Wait!" He walked to the dining room door, opened it and went in.

Maria was behind the front desk, placid, pale and inscrutable. Her large, bright eyes followed him as he came in and she pursed her lips faintly. De Vincenzi advanced, quickly taking in the group of tables. They were all full, and at almost every one of them he saw men gambling. Yet not a word could be heard. The cards were slapped down on the green baize and picked up by mute robots. A woman in mourning, her elbows on the table, gazed into space. De Vincenzi saw some other women. Their eyes were so bright and staring it seemed as if they were all hallucinating. The air in the room was thick with cigarette smoke—and with terror. A creepy, indescribable terror that bore down on all of them. Thus oppressed, they kept quiet and played.

45

Suddenly a hoarse voice was heard.

"A five and four kings…"

Everyone turned. The voice came from a corner table where two men sat facing one another, their cards fanned out in their hands. A third, sitting beside them, was keeping score in the notebook he had in front of him.

"I said, a five of diamonds and four kings… What? Good, right?"

He was an elephantine character, with a pointy head sunk between two shoulders rounded like the lid of a trunk. His huge body, ridiculously perched on a chair too small for him, slumped over, solid and bulky. De Vincenzi looked at him in profile. The man was staring at his cards with small, bleary eyes under his huge greying thicket of eyebrows. His earlobes were heavy and red like wattles and his nose jutted out imposingly above purplish lips. It seemed as if he'd been modelled in grey clay and set out to dry in the sun.

He began to put the cards down slowly, one after the other, each gesture accompanied by a loud huffing that distended his lips with every puff. A mischievous, mocking smile flitted through the bright eyes and over the fleshy lips of the opponent sitting across from him. It had gone quiet again and, for a few more minutes, everything around them was still. It seemed as if the projector had stopped, with the figures on the screen frozen mid-gesture: a foot raised, a hand held out, a face at three-quarter view. Then someone let out a deep sigh and the figures moved. The machine had resumed its movement.

De Vincenzi turned on his heel and went back into the lobby. "Ask the proprietor to come and see me."

Virgilio was trembling and flapping about in order to control

46

his panic. He cast a pitiful look at the inspector, his round eyes bulging from his head.

"How long had Douglas Layng been in your hotel?"

"A month… a month…"

"Which room?"

"Number 5, on the first floor."

"Did he eat in the hotel?"

"Yes."

"And did he eat breakfast here today—or should I say yesterday, since it's now past midnight?"

The hotel manager struck his forehead with his hand.

"But of course! You're making me think, now. He didn't come down to breakfast today; his table was empty. In fact, I said as much to my wife and she replied that he'd probably gone to see some village near the lakes. Over the past few days, I recall him mentioning that he was going to take some excursions. He could only stay in Italy a few weeks longer and wanted to see as much as possible. Absolutely—I remember it perfectly now."

"So neither you nor your wife bothered to send someone to see if he was still in his room?"

"No. It's true, we didn't. But why would we think of doing that? In any case, wasn't it that evening he was killed?"

De Vincenzi went on with his questions.

"Did your wife see him go out that morning?"

"I don't know. I doubt it. She would have told me."

If he had to, he'd question that stony woman behind the desk later and watch her lose some of her imperturbable calm. It was better to wrap things up with her husband for now.

"Who lives in the rooms on the top floor?"

"You mean… where the bo—"

"Of course."

"Oh! Carlo Da Como in the one at the end… in the first one, Signor Engel."

"A foreigner?" He was thinking about that doll.

"Yes… no… I mean, he must be German, but he's been in Italy for years."

"And this Carlo Da Como?"

"From Milan. He has family here. He was rich, but now…"

"Now?"

"He manages to keep going. But he's a gentleman. He's looking for some occupation. Commendatore Besesti has promised him a position in his bank."

"Are they in there, those two? In the dining room?"

"Yes, they're gambling. See? The ones playing piquet. There are three of them, along with Captain Lontario. He was injured in the war. Very respectable, really, comes every evening, lives with his mother. Yes, a real gentleman."

"Enough about the captain! What about the other two rooms?"

"Which? Oh, yes. Mario—the factotum—sleeps in the first one. There he is, behind the counter. The two maids sleep in the other one. Sisters, from the same village as my mother."

"Who found the body?"

"Bardi, the hunchback. He sells watches. He's lived in this hotel for at least ten years. He was here when I took over the business, and he feels at home here, although his intrusiveness sometimes bothers me. Not to say… But the fact is that with the old owners he was almost like family."

"Which is his room?"

"Number 19, at the end of the second corridor."

"And what was he doing on the top floor? What reason would he have had for going up there?"

"Reason?" The man smiled in that slimy, unctuous way of his. "But that man never has any reason for sticking his nose into everyone's business. Who knows why he took it into his head to go up there? He knows everything that goes on in here. He must have wanted to spy on the maids."

So the hunchback knew everything that went on in the hotel: *the devil is grinning from every corner…*

"Does this Bardi have a typewriter?"

"How did you know? He does, in fact."

"Is he the only person to have one in the hotel?"

"I can't say for sure. I just manage the restaurant, right? It's my wife who looks after the rooms. You can ask her or the maids. Bardi has a typewriter—it's a really old one, and he's the only one who can actually manage to write with it—that much I know, because from time to time he'll type something for me."

This, perhaps, was a point gained, and easy to confirm straightaway. He had the anonymous letter in his pocket. But he held back. It would be significant only if Bardi consented to tell everything he knew. Maybe he'd speak more freely if he didn't think anyone was fingering him as the author of that strange missive. But why, after all, would he have written it? Well, given his sort, there wasn't really any need to look for a reason. *Some hysterical woman*, he'd immediately thought. And if the letter had really been written by that unfortunate man, he hadn't been far off. He looked at the hotelier.

"There's all-night gambling in your hotel."

"Oh, we're all one big family! No one plays for much."

"Is that right? We'll talk later about this gambling for small beer. Right now, go and send Signor Bardi to me."

Virgilio vacillated somewhat, as if building up the momentum to move.

"He'll hardly want to come, you know. If you make me close the hotel, it'll ruin me!"

"Go and do what I asked."

The man moved on, his eyes bulging more than ever. Through the glass, De Vincenzi saw him go into the dining room and walk towards the back. Only two guests lived upstairs: Carlo Da Como and Vilfredo Engel. That macabre *mise en scène* was therefore the work of one of those two. Which one?

Slowly dragging legs disproportionately long for his child-like body, the hunchback Bardi reached the wicker table and stood in the light of the rosy lamp.

"Sit down," De Vincenzi said affably. Bardi sat down immediately. He must have felt his legs giving way. "You were the first to see the body and to raise the alarm, is that right?"

"Yes."

"Why did you go all the way upstairs? Your own room is in another part of the building entirely."

It was the last question the hunchback expected at that moment. Why had he gone up there? He looked almost ashen. His nose was thin, sharp and so delicate round the nostrils as to seem like transparent membrane. His nostrils were quivering. But the fact that he had no eyelashes at all was simultaneously comic and disconcerting. His troubled grey eyes appeared to issue from two holes, without any support; they were naked. His entire face, for that matter, was so smooth, so furrowed with tiny lines at his temples and the corners of his mouth as to give the impression of an almost obscene nudity.

"Why did I go upstairs?" He was panting. He must have been suffering from asthma, like almost everyone with a thoracic deformity. "I wanted to… It's hardly a crime for me to have gone up there… I wanted to…"

He was searching, and desperately—though without success—for an acceptable lie. He was a sly one. In ordinary circumstances he'd never have hesitated so much, but he'd received an extreme shock. It had literally driven him mad.

"Signor Bardi, very strange things are going on in this hotel. Did you expect to find a dead man when you went upstairs?"

"What are you talking about?"

"A dead man... or woman?"

"What are you saying?"

Were his bright eyes dancing with terror, or was it only indignant surprise?

"Did you know young Layng well?"

A vague gesture. "He hardly spoke. All the more so because he couldn't yet express himself correctly in Italian. And for several days he did nothing but play cards. Someone taught him to play baccarat and he caught the gambling bug."

"Did he lose?"

"A lot. Too much."

"So he had money?"

"Poor man! He received ten pounds a month from London. Or so he told me. He was a methodical young man, careful to the last cent. He'd ask the price of every dish before ordering it. It was obvious that this was the first time he'd been away from his family, from his... *mamma*. He must have been brought up well; he had sound moral principles. And then—"

He interrupted himself, wetting his lips with his tongue.

"Go on."

"The other night, he lost more than a thousand lire."

"Did he pay up?"

"The next day, with a cheque drawn on the Banca Commerciale. He came down to the dining room at midday holding the cheque. Before he handed it over he asked his creditor if… if it would be possible for him to pay only half. He was all choked up and seemed ready to cry."

"What about his creditor?"

"He replied that in Italy gambling debts are debts of honour and honour is non-negotiable. Idiot!"

He was outraged, and his long, monkey-like hands trembled on very thin wrists.

"To whom did he give the cheque?"

Bardi hesitated. He looked at De Vincenzi with a sardonic smile. "Does that have anything to do with the murder? You're questioning me about matters relating to the crime. As for the rest, I am obliged neither to know anything nor to tell you what I know," he said with a wicked smirk.

"I'll find out in any case, whether you tell me or not."

"That's as may be. It's easy enough. But if I reveal it, they'll call me a gossip. They already accuse me of being an old woman. And then, why should I help you find out about all these people here? Why me? Ask them about their criminal records. You'll learn a lot."

He laughed like a naughty, spiteful child. If De Vincenzi hadn't asked him the question, he might have come out with it himself. He was upset about the dead man because he was dead. But he hated the living because he was a hunchback with an inferiority complex who was always having to suffer humiliations from his peers.

"Will I also learn that *a gathering of addicts and degenerates* meets here?"

Bardi held the inspector's gaze without lowering his eyes. "I don't know what you mean."

But he knew all right. The letter was undoubtedly his.

"So you didn't know, either, that *the devil is grinning from every corner of that house.*"

He shrugged. "Just words…" But he was shaking.

"Signor Bardi, anyone who withholds from the law information in his possession is considered complicit in a crime and will be liable to serious precautionary and coercive measures."

"What do you know about what I know?"

"Was there someone here with whom Douglas Layng was particularly friendly?"

"You mean, his killer? If only I could imagine who killed him in that way."

"How do you think the young man was killed?"

"What the deuce! He was hanged! I saw him."

"You saw a body hanging from a rope. But Douglas Layng was killed by a stab in the back. Someone hung up his body, and they did so at least fifteen or sixteen hours after he died."

"No…" He seemed deflated. He put his head between his hands, trembling all over. "It's terrible! Oh…" He wasn't feigning.

De Vincenzi got up and went over to stand beside him. "Yes, it's terrible. That's why you must help me find his killer. Do you want another crime to be committed here? Tell me everything you know."

Bardi leapt to his feet, holding his hands in front of him as if to defend himself.

"I don't know anything! I don't know anything!" he shouted. His voice, normally frail and reedy, was now louder and sounded cracked and shrill. "I don't know anything! Leave me in peace, for pity's sake!"

He ran towards the dining room, seeking refuge once more in the far corner near the piquet table.

"Shall I go and get him?" Sani asked.

"Let him go. He'll speak before tomorrow morning."

De Vincenzi had decided not to let those people rest, not even for a second. Perhaps he'd push someone to do something crazy—the circle in which they were moving was already red-hot and the atmosphere rising to white heat—but he would uncover the truth, whatever the cost.

An athletic youth with wide, square shoulders, narrow waist and massive legs appeared at the door. His light-grey suit of fine, brushed fabric hugged his sculpted form, and his tie was a bright flame-red. With strong, regular features and a short black moustache, his face instantly seemed common.

He stopped on the threshold and looked around the lobby with a faint but marked sense of surprise. He then turned towards the dining room and saw Maria's calm, unruffled face. He shrugged slightly, as if none of his observations made any sense, and went in.

De Vincenzi watched him. Sani moved towards him in order to stop him, and the officer on guard beside the door raised his hand.

So the youth stopped again. He looked at the deputy inspector.

"Please?"

"Where are you going?"

He answered in poor Italian, and with a strong American accent. "To lie down."

"Who are you?"

He smiled. "Police?"

"Exactly."

"Nicola Al Righetti."

Sani had been questioning him, and he now turned expectantly to De Vincenzi.

54

"Mr Al Righetti, would you sit here with me for a minute or two? Let's chat."

Why had he adopted his most kindly and good-natured attitude when he didn't even like this youth? One of the five on the list Bianchi had given him. Al Righetti went over to the table, took the chair Bardi had been sitting in, moved it away slightly and sat down.

"I don't like to disturb guests at a hotel, keep them from their usual routines, but I must. Have you heard?"

"About what?"

"You must have heard, right? About the murder…"

The other man interrupted him. "Is this about a murder? If you're going the long way round to get me to fall into some trap, you can save yourself the trouble. I don't know anything apart from this: I was eating peacefully in there—I ask to be served in the billiard room where it's quieter—and I heard shouting, plates falling, chairs being overturned. I thought the customers were fighting and I stayed put. Pietro, the waiter, told me someone had been hanged, the young Englishman. Then the police came. I stopped eating and left the billiard room to go to bed. That's it."

"Ah, naturally! If that's all, then what you know isn't of much help to us. Where are you from, Mr Al Righetti?"

"I'm from Paris. Or rather, New York. But I disembarked at Marseilles and went to Paris for a few days. From Paris, via Geneva to Milan."

"Why Milan?"

"Why not? I like Italy."

"What do you do? That is, what is your profession?"

"None." He took his time, rubbing his hands vigorously. He pulled out his wallet and showed De Vincenzi a stack of banknotes. "See?" He put the wallet back in his pocket and tossed his passport on the table in front of the inspector.

"My passport's in order. I have money. What else do you need?"

De Vincenzi picked up the passport and offered it to Sani. "Take this and put it with the others we'll be collecting." He then turned back to the American and said with the utmost affability, "All of this would certainly be enough if there hadn't been a murder in the hotel you're staying in."

"What does the murder have to do with me? How could I possibly be involved? I came down from my room at seven and stayed in that room to talk to Mr Da Como, one of the guests, until around eight. Then I went out, because I usually eat late in the evenings, and I went to the Biffi Bar in the Galleria. Everyone there knows me and you can check up on my statement. I stayed in the bar till around ten. I came back here, went straight to the billiard room, ordered something to eat, and on account of the interruption caused by—that incident—I stopped eating only then. How could I have killed young Layng? You tell me! My alibi is rock-solid."

So he was talking about alibis… Even if De Vincenzi hadn't known from the information Bianchi had gathered that Al Righetti normally lived in Chicago, he would have guessed it from the way he was dealing with this police interrogation.

"And what were you doing from eleven this morning till seven?"

"You want to know that too?" But there was something more than surprise in his voice. "At eleven I was in my room sleeping, or nearly. I was in bed, in any case. I came down after twelve, ate and went out. I didn't come back until six. I can provide an alibi for all that time too if necessary." If he'd lost his certainty, he'd recovered it.

"Did you know Douglas Layng?"

"Know him? I saw him here in the hotel, of course, and we may have spoken. Nothing more."

"That's fine. That'll be enough for now. Go ahead and rest."

Al Righetti got up. "One of the things I hate most is to be woken from a sound sleep."

"We'll see to it that you're left alone—until tomorrow morning."

"Thank you."

When he got to the bottom of the stairs, he heard the inspector's voice: "Mr Al Righetti, do you know the lawyer Flemington?"

He turned, laughing softly.

"Bravo. The loaded question for last! But I've never heard of your—this lawyer Flemington."

And he slowly began to climb the stairs, disappearing after the first landing.

7

Room 5 was the first on the left at the start of the corridor, immediately after the spacious landing.

De Vincenzi had a moment of hesitation as he put his hand to the brass doorknob. But he shrugged his shoulders and, smiling sceptically at Sani, grasped the handle. "This isn't a fingerprints sort of crime, and if I phoned forensics at this hour, they'd think I was mad!"

The window was wide open, and both men shivered as they went in. It was still raining outside and fog had entered the room, so when they flipped the switch, the light from the lamp looked veiled and gave off a smoky halo.

"Close it. What does this window look out on?"

"The courtyard." Sani bit back a curse—there was a little table in front of the window and, leaning out, he'd caught his finger in the shutters.

A small white bed… it was the first thing De Vincenzi saw. It looked as if the sheets and bedcover had been pulled right over the pillow, but the bed had not been remade. Someone had simply covered it like that. He pulled back the edge of the sheet. Exactly what he'd expected.

However, he could never have imagined such a horrible sight. God, how the young man had bled. The blood must have soaked through the mattress. A pair of white pyjamas, hidden under the blankets at the foot of the bed, were also dark with blood. Someone had torn them off the victim after the killing and they'd served to staunch the wound and then to rub the body dry. He quickly pulled the covers up again.

The modus operandi now appeared all too clear. But why hadn't the killer feared being surprised by one of the maids? If the doctor's calculations were correct, the young man had been killed yesterday morning, or in the early hours of the previous night. He would verify Layng's movements from four in the afternoon until he'd gone to the dining room, probably to gamble. They'd given him a passion for baccarat—it was in his blood—and they'd been fleecing him. A thousand lire in one go, for someone who had to live on ten pounds a month, was really a sensational loss. Who'd gained from it? He would find out, but then what? One thing seemed certain: that the person who'd won the money was not the killer. You don't strangle the goose that lays the golden eggs… Unless young Layng had noticed that such a person was cheating and had threatened to expose him, insisting that the money for his debt be returned to him, and then that person had shut him up for ever. The theory was plausible. Plausible, but foolish in this particular case. It didn't square with the macabre *mise en scène* featuring the hanged man. Not at all. Things couldn't have been that simple, and it couldn't have been the motive for the crime.

De Vincenzi's mind was wandering. He took up the thread again. Layng, therefore, had been killed at an unspecified time on Monday morning, and in any case not later than early afternoon, even if the doctor was mistaken. So how could the body have been kept hidden in that room without anyone discovering it? Was it credible that the maid had not entered the room all day, that no one had noticed Douglas's disappearance or gone to look for him? He hadn't gone down to breakfast. No one had seen him, as usual, and no one was worried about it. But even allowing that this was actually the case, how could the killer have made his calculations *before* it happened, and how could he have been so confident as to risk the stabbing?

De Vincenzi's gaze lingered over the small bedside tray with its empty cup and small spoon. Someone had brought him a coffee in his room. He held the cup, wrinkling his brow. It had been carefully washed—there was no residue. Therefore? Therefore, a narcotic or some poison must have been added to the coffee. Simple. And the killer had taken care to rinse the cup. An unnecessary precaution, as it happened. The autopsy…

Sani was rummaging in the suitcase, in the trunk, in the drawers. Nothing of any interest. Everything was very tidy. The undergarments were those of someone who was comfortably off. A silver shaving kit.

"Look how he kept the letters he received." Sani pointed to the top dresser drawer, where there was a packet of letters still in their envelopes, tied with a ribbon. He picked them up and went through them. "They're from England. They must be from his parents."

"I'll look at them later," said De Vincenzi, and he pressed the bell.

Sani gazed at him in surprise. "Who do you think will come up? They're all locked in the dining room, being guarded by the officer."

"You're right. Go and get the two maids and the porter. I believe there's one of those in this hotel."

Sani went out and left the door open. De Vincenzi followed him into the corridor. There, at least, the lamps shone brightly. At the end, the corridor turned round a corner. He counted two doors on the same side as Room 5 and four on the opposite side. The line of doors continued down the other part of the corridor. Just in front of Room 5 was Room 1. Beside it, Room 6. The numbering went up to 4 on the right and continued with 5 on the left.

He went over to the landing, leant over the balustrade and called the officer standing guard at the bottom of the stairs.

"Have the owner give you a plan of the hotel with everyone's names and room numbers. Understood?"

"Yes, sir."

Sani returned with the two chambermaids and the porter. De Vincenzi went back into the room where Layng had been killed. The others followed. The maids were haggard, yellowed miseries, ageless, almost sexless. Sisters, the manager said, from his mother's own village. It was obvious that they were from the country. They came into the room slowly and circumspectly, as if urged on by the big, dark-haired young man behind them in shirtsleeves and a turquoise-striped apron.

"Which of you works on this floor?"

"Both of us," the taller one answered. Her nose was long and yellow like a duck's beak. "This is the only floor."

"What about the rooms upstairs?"

"Oh, those! We do those when we finish down here, sometimes even in the evenings."

"So yesterday morning you were both on this floor?"

"All three of us," the porter interrupted. "I was with them. We do the rooms together."

"Who brings coffee to the rooms?"

"Whoever. When someone rings, whoever is closest to the room responds."

"Try hard to remember: which of you three brought coffee to Signor Layng in this room yesterday morning?"

The two girls looked at each other but didn't hesitate.

"She did," said the first one to speak.

"I did," confirmed the other.

"At what time?"

"It must have been eight."

"Did he ring?"

"Yes."

"How did you find him?"

"In bed, as usual."

"Was he awake?"

"Of course. He told me to open the shutters."

"Did he ring every morning at eight?"

"Yes."

"You got the coffee downstairs. Where?"

"Well, at the counter. Mario made the coffee in the machine, one by one as we ordered them."

"And you brought it straight up here?"

The woman seemed confused. She had no idea what the coffee had to do with it.

"Yes, of course."

"Think carefully! You took the coffee from Mario's hands and brought it here."

"Well, of course."

"You're sure of that?"

Her sister and the porter looked at her. They, too, were bemused.

"Absolutely. What do you mean?"

"I'm asking if you're absolutely certain that you didn't put the tray down somewhere before taking it to Signor Layng... if you were called to some other room."

"I don't think so. I remember having brought two trays, one

62

with a full breakfast and black coffee for Room 1 and the other with a black coffee for Room 5."

"And?"

"Oh yes! I put the tray for Room 5 on the table on the landing, out there, and went into Room 1. Then I picked it up again and came in here."

"How long did you stay in Room 1?"

"Only a couple of minutes—just to open the window, give the cup of coffee to the *signore* and put the breakfast tray on the *signora's* nightstand."

"Who's staying in Room 1?"

"A journalist and his wife."

The intense questioning continued. The two women and the man spoke with evident sincerity, but they didn't know anything. The coffee tray, therefore, had remained for a few minutes on the table on the landing. Was that when the killer—or an accomplice—had dropped in a sleeping tablet? A sleeping tablet, or poison? But they could set aside the possibility of poison, since there would then have been no need for the stabbing.

Had they seen the Englishman leave his room?

No, not one of the three had seen him.

"Why didn't one of you come into this room to clean it?"

"But we did come in, sir," exclaimed the taller of the sisters, who must have been the elder.

De Vincenzi started. "You came in here? Which one of you?"

"I did," the woman replied, "and Luigi." The porter agreed.

"What time was it?"

"How should I know? It would have been sometime around eleven… must have been a bit later, but definitely before noon. We'd finished all the other rooms. The door to Room 5 was closed. I knocked, then opened the door. The room was empty. We cleaned it and left, closing the door as usual."

If those two weren't lying—and it was unlikely they were—Douglas Layng had not yet been killed by eleven. But in that case…

"Just a minute here," De Vincenzi shouted impatiently. "How can you have cleaned up in here if the tray and the coffee cup are still there on the nightstand?" All three turned to look at the objects. All three showed signs of the greatest surprise. No one spoke for several moments. Then Luigi shrugged.

"It must have been brought up later—in the afternoon."

"By whom? Which one of you remembers having brought it to him?"

Not one of them remembered doing so. The two women and the porter insisted in no uncertain terms and with every appearance of truth that they hadn't seen the Englishman at all that day. No, they hadn't gone into his room again; they'd had no reason to do so. And the evening? Yes, the chambermaids had gone into some rooms between eight and nine to turn down the beds; but not in all of them, and almost never in Layng's, and in any case not that evening.

De Vincenzi was about to continue his questioning when the officer he'd sent for the hotel plan appeared at the door with several sheets in his hand. He seemed bashful.

"So? Give them here."

The officer held out the papers. "One of the people in the locked room downstairs is asking to speak with you right away. He seems obsessed and he set to, making the devil of a racket, screaming that it smacks of a veritable imprisonment of his person, he has nothing to do with the crime, he has an urgent appointment…"

"Who is it?"

"I don't know. He's a thin, gangly sort, dark as an Abyssinian." The two women laughed. "He's the one with all the tricks."

"He's a chiromancer who predicts the future."

De Vincenzi knew that he was a sales rep for articles from the bazaar, of German make. He kept them in a suitcase, always ready to show his astonishing tricks to the first person to stumble by: ducklings gliding over water, shells that bloomed in water with branches of coral, meadow flowers that turned into pink piglets when inflated. But what really drew the girls was the magical quality of his person. He was a palm-reader—a chiromancer, they said—able to predict the future. And he must also have been a hypnotist, because "when he stared into a woman's eyes, she'd fall asleep". Not one of the three could say where he came from, but they all agreed he couldn't be Italian.

"Fine," De Vincenzi cut in. "Bring him up." He sent the two chambermaids and the porter back downstairs, convinced they'd told him everything they knew… maybe. Maybe. Because the coffee story was completely inexplicable at the moment. The young man had undoubtedly been killed in his own bed, in that room. But when?

Sani looked at his watch. "It's two," he said quietly. "I'm wondering…"

"What?"

"… if we can continue to keep these people locked in the dining room all night."

De Vincenzi shrugged. "They're playing cards, just like every other night."

A voice from downstairs said: "The inspector is on the first floor." They heard someone coming up.

It was the doctor. He was very tall, and with his hat pulled down over his eyes, his collar turned up and a long nose that stuck out menacingly like a beak, he looked more like a scare-crow than ever.

"I've finished. You can order him to be moved to the Monumentale cemetery. I'll go there tomorrow morning for the autopsy." He was ready to leave.

"You can't tell me anything else, then?"

"What do you want me to tell you? Someone killed him. The weapon must have been a long, thin knife, pushed in right up to the hilt. The rope used to hang him left bruises, but they weren't very deep, which means that, hung up like so, he would have been there less than an hour."

"When did he die?"

"It'll be necessary to find out where the body was kept until he was hung up. If it was a very warm place, then rigor mortis wouldn't have lasted as long and the secondary flaccidity, which in this particular case had barely started, would have appeared fifteen or sixteen hours after death. Normally it manifests twenty-four hours later."

"Taking into account that he was kept in this room or a similar one..."

The doctor grunted in assent and looked around. "And you took him down when?"

"Around eleven-thirty, or thereabouts."

"OK. I'd say he was killed sometime around nine or ten in the morning. There you go." He turned on his heel and disappeared.

Sani looked at De Vincenzi. "At eleven the chambermaid and porter came to the room and the body wasn't here!"

"Right. But go on. We're not finished!"

"Eh? The sheets weren't yet soaked with blood at eleven."

"Right. And at eleven, that rinsed cup wasn't on the night-stand. Therefore, according to all appearances, which might be certainties, Douglas Layng hadn't yet drunk the narcotic and was still alive."

"And yet the doctor couldn't have been out by four hours. Post-mortem indications don't lie."

"Hmm. He said himself: if he was kept in a very warm place…" De Vincenzi looked around and went over to touch the radiator elements: warm, yes, but not enough to be suffocating. He opened the wardrobe: nothing but clothes. He was looking for something and not finding it.

Sani followed his movements, clearly uneasy. "What are you looking for?"

De Vincenzi didn't reply. He walked around the room once more, then suddenly stopped and sniffed the air.

"The window was open, yes?"

"Wide open."

"Ah!"

That could be the explanation. In which case, his hunch stood up. Everything now hinged on whether or not he'd find in some other room what he'd vainly looked for in this one, ever since the discovery. There wouldn't have been enough time to take something so cumbersome out of the hotel. Unless… What did he actually know about what had happened from the time they'd found the body until Bianchi had arrived with his officers, considering that Bianchi had immediately blocked all exits?

"Here he is, Inspector."

The officer presented a skeletal man dressed entirely in black, his bony face ashen, the colour olive-toned skins turn when they pale. The blackest of eyes flamed out from their sunken sockets.

"Ah! What's your name?"

"Giorgio Novarreno."

De Vincenzi was ready to begin his interrogation, but the man slowly and solemnly raised his right hand, forcing De Vincenzi to keep quiet. He remained absolutely still, but quickly scanned the entire room.

"A man was killed in this room," he offered, his voice warm and melodious, "at precisely twelve-thirty yesterday. There's still a lot of blood in here."

Sani flinched. De Vincenzi wasted no time; he took his subordinate by the arm and pushed him out of the door.

"Wait for me downstairs."

He closed the door once more, turned the key in the lock and put it in his pocket. He then went to stand in front of the palm-reader, who remained fixed in his moment of inspiration.

"No play-acting," De Vincenzi stated, placing a hand on his shoulder. "Tell me everything you know—or else I'll immediately accuse you of being the author of this crime or an accomplice."

8

The man gave no sign of being uneasy. Whether it was remarkable self-control and a seasoned talent for acting or he really did believe in his own supernatural strength, he maintained his moment of rapture.

"You can't accuse me of a crime that was committed by someone else."

"By whom?"

He smiled, and his smile was sinister. "I don't deny that someone might be able to find out. I don't know."

"I repeat: this is not a performance. So you can begin by telling me something about yourself. What do you do?"

"Salesman. Everyone knows it…" He paused, then seemed to become human. He spoke simply, as if confiding in someone. "I'm a salesman *now*. I've had a lively existence, I have. I've been all over the world, earning my keep with some effort. I come from the East. In Italy, Levantines are not known for their honesty." He shrugged. "You won't find anyone who can make a well-founded accusation against me. What have I done? I've grown and sold tobacco; I've been a stoker on the Sea of Azov; fisherman on the Black Sea; I've traded in bricks and watermelons, going up and down the Dnieper; I've been a clown in a circus; I was an actor. Now? I deal in trifles. Indispensable objects—because they're unnecessary. Men don't always need bread, but they always need someone to make them marvel. A little paper flower, which opens as if by magic…"

On a night like this, after having taken a body down from a rope, De Vincenzi's nerves were raw. But he controlled himself. If there were some way to get this cunning and deceitful Levantine to reveal something useful, he could do nothing but let him go on talking in his own way, and do all the acting he wished.

Novarreno had taken a step backward and had gone still again. A smile crept over the inspector's face and he went to sit with his back to the wall.

"Take a seat. I believe we'll be speaking for some time."

A look of dismay flitted over Novarreno's ashen face. "In here?" He looked around, and his gaze fell on the headboard. "I actually have some urgent business… an appointment."

"At this hour? Are you joking, Novarreno? It'll soon be three in the morning. Sit down, I tell you, and let's talk about this calmly. I'm not in a hurry myself. I'm not leaving this hotel until I find out who killed Douglas Layng—and until I've arrested him, of course."

"But what do I have to do with it? I don't know anything."

"You know, for example, that the young man was killed in this room and that he was killed at exactly twelve-thirty. You said so yourself! And you're the only one who knows this. I'll bet that—" He jumped up and turned back the bedcover and the sheets, revealing a huge stain, black with blood. "Look! Did you know this, too?"

Novarreno didn't even back away. Angry and stock-still, he looked beyond the stain at the headboard… Only his jaw muscles worked convulsively, as if he were using incredible force to control himself.

"I know nothing! I sensed that a man had been killed in here as soon as I entered this room."

"Ah, yes! So you're a necromancer, right? And the time it happened? Did you feel that, too, when you came into the room?"

"Yes," and he added no more. He didn't even try to make it seem logical, to offer an explanation, to justify his absurd claim with an argument, however specious.

But why had he spoken? It didn't seem possible that he was the killer, for the precise reason that he'd talked. However great an actor he was, however consumed with the need to cause continual sensation—to shock—one could not suppose that the charlatan in him was stronger than his sense of danger, his instinct for self-preservation. And since one couldn't give any weight to his necromantic divination—even if one tried to explain it as a hypersensitivity of the nerves or a telepathic phenomenon—what was left?

"Where is your room, Novarreno?"

"Next to this one. The next door along."

De Vincenzi was left, therefore, simply with this: the Levantine had heard Douglas Layng being killed through the thin walls of his room and now, after having impulsively and rashly given in to his desire to demonstrate his occult and divinatory powers, he was reluctant to speak for fear of the killer.

For the third time, De Vincenzi said curtly: "Sit down!" and the man sat in a chair beside the bed, without showing the least horror or repugnance at the blood-soaked sheets. The inspector covered up the bed again—he was the one who couldn't stand the sight.

"Listen to me closely, Giorgio Novarreno. Don't imagine that I'm going to let this farce continue. You know something,

71

and you've got to tell me what you know. You won't be leaving this room until you've talked. Understood?"

The man shook his head. "I don't know a thing."

"What were you doing, and where were you yesterday at half past twelve?"

A malicious smile was the first response; it came to him spontaneously. He spoke slowly.

"Was I the only one to give you the time of the crime? Or had you already more or less settled on that moment?"

"What if I told you that my calculations and those of the doctor coincided exactly with your information?"

"I'd have to believe you. But I remain struck by it as I would by a supernatural event. Think about it, I beg you. If I were the killer or his accomplice, it's obvious that even if I were play-acting, as you say, I would have suggested any time except that of the crime, and in any case I would have proposed a time for which I had an alibi. So either you believe that I've spoken moved by some force outside myself—call it telepathy, occultism, divination, the nervous tension of a sick organism, whatever you wish, in fact—in which case you're trying to prove a suggestion that might be completely wrong... or you believe that I might be mixed up in this business, in which case you should pay no heed to my words and consider them no more than a guilty man's attempt to derail your investigation and confuse your thoughts."

He was clever. In command of himself, in any case. Of course there had to be something else underneath all this. This man, acting as he did, was clearly pursuing his own goal. But what was it?

All at once, De Vincenzi decided to change tactic and rely on cunning. "That's right," he said. "I see you're not devoid of logic. But you could be helpful to me all the same and I'm counting on your voluntary collaboration."

"Of course."

"When did you see Douglas Layng for the last time?"

"Yesterday morning."

"What time?"

"Three in the morning, when we came upstairs together to go to bed."

"Who else was with you?"

"I don't know. I only remember coming up with Layng. The others had either gone up before us or followed later. The game was over."

"With whom had the Englishman been playing?"

"With everyone... baccarat isn't a closed game, you know. Donato Desatta was banker and anyone who wanted to placed a bet."

"And the Englishman?"

"From the moment he learnt how to play that cursed game, he played whenever he could, like a desperate man. In the early evening, when he had no alternatives, he'd start playing baccarat with only one other player. He even played with the ladies."

"And lost."

"Yes."

"Who taught him how to play?"

Novarreno didn't hesitate. "Da Como." He smiled. "Da Como will be hit hardest of all by his death."

So Carlo Da Como was the one who'd won a thousand lire in one night with Layng. And he was living in one of the little rooms on the top floor... Was it possible to imagine that the tragic *mise en scène* had been staged just for him?

"What did you and Layng talk about when you went upstairs?"

"Nothing. A few words, whatever one says on the way to bed after sitting shut up in a room for hours, gambling."

He was lying. De Vincenzi could tell that he was lying. Even if his hesitation hadn't been obvious before he spoke, his actual voice, which he'd tried to infuse with indifference, had betrayed him. But why? He was clearly responding to some of the questions with sincerity, though there were others he was trying to avoid.

"Where were you born, Novarreno?"

"In Adalia. On the Gulf of Adalia, across from Cyprus... Asiatic Turkey. A miserable, tragic country."

"How long have you been in Italy?"

"Since '14."

"And during the war?"

"I travelled... on behalf of your government."

So he'd been a spy, if one could believe he was telling the truth. It would be easy to check.

"Yesterday? Tell me what you were doing from—from, shall we say, eight in the morning onwards."

"If you want me to give you an alibi you can check up on, I don't think I've got one. For the very reason that I could never have imagined that what's happened would happen, I took no steps to ensure that I had one."

"Let's see... before we come back to this, how did you know Douglas Layng had been killed?"

"The hunchback yelled it out to everyone. How could I have failed to hear? I was by myself in the lobby, tucked away in a corner. I often go off on my own because I need to think freely. Bardi went by, running and screaming: 'There's a hanged man' or something like that. There was a moment of panic... women fainting... chairs overturned... Someone found the nerve to go and look."

74

"Who?"

"Me. And I was the one who telephoned the police."

"So you saw the dead man. What then?"

"Then—nothing!"

"On the contrary, then everything, because everything must have led you to suppose that the young man had been killed yesterday evening. You saw him hanging. So why did you say, as soon as you came in here, that the murder had been committed at twelve-thirty?"

He didn't miss a beat.

"I could say I don't know, because when I'm speaking during a state of spiritual clairvoyance, or something near it, I'm unaware of what I'm saying. And yet I'll tell you that, precisely because I did see the hanged man, I was convinced that the crime had been committed some time earlier, and that the rope and all the rest were nothing but a trick rigged up to scare someone."

"Ah, so you're a medical expert now?"

"Somewhat. Of course, I've seen many bodies in my life. The Armenian massacres, the Great Thessaloniki Fire…"

"So you thought *the trick was rigged up to scare someone.* Who?"

He shrugged. "How should I know?"

"What about your clairvoyant powers?"

"My clairvoyance is limited to calculating which people, last night or this morning, would have had to bump into the body to believe there was one. But you can make that sort of calculation on your own."

"You're right. So yesterday at twelve-thirty, you were…"

"I was in the Galleria when the midday siren sounded. I started slowly for the hotel… I would have reached it in fifteen or twenty minutes."

"And you naturally came up to your room?"

"No. I went into the dining room and sat down at my table to eat."

"Who else was in the dining room at that time?"

"Well, let's see… I can remember if I try. Signor Belloni—the cashier of the Banca Indigena—his whole family were there: his wife and daughter… Agresti, with his wife… Desatta and Vittoria were there… You know who Vittoria is, don't you?… And then that American… the Nolan woman… and the actress Stella Essington… and everyone in the usual group of old men—they have the table at the back and don't live in the hotel—and then… yes, Da Como and Engel came in a bit later… and before one, Pompeo Besesti, the owner of the Bank of Pure Metals. Do you know him? They say he's a fairly rich man. That's it. Of course, none of this is worth anything as a witness statement. My memory may betray me. I was thinking about eating, not busy checking the hotel register to see who was missing. Not to mention that in no restaurant in the world are the diners always the same."

"That afternoon, you didn't go up to your room?"

"No, not until last night at eight. I went out right after lunch and didn't come back to the hotel."

"Where were you?"

"Another alibi entirely lacking witnesses… Every morning before I leave my room, I do my daily horoscope in order to find out how best to comport myself and how to go about my business. Well, yesterday my horoscope was dire."

He took a notebook from his pocket, opened it and read:

> *A profusion of malign influences thanks to the Moon's configuration with Uranus and Neptune. A day of difficult events and sinister complications.*

He lifted his head and looked at De Vincenzi. "Do you want to read it? I wrote these lines yesterday morning."

"Fine, fine." The inspector was condescending. "Another amazing divination. But I don't see—"

"—what my horoscope has to do with my alibi for yesterday afternoon? How can I simplify this... A bad horoscope for me means no business prospects. And in those cases I don't try to do anything. For that reason, I left my suitcase in the hotel yesterday, the one with all my—frivolous—samples in it, and went to Lake Como. I left from the North station on the 2.40 and came back on the train that arrives in Milan at 7.20. That's it. There's no hope, however, of anyone being able to confirm my statement, unless... of course... unless the North station ticket-seller at the window for Como remembers my face and the fact that I gave him a five-hundred-lire note to pay for a return ticket when it was only ten lire in total. He was very put out."

Cleverer than ever. The alibi? Novarreno had one, and how. And it was one of those alibis that appear all the more genuine for being apparently casual and totally unprepared. If he were to find himself in a tight spot, that Levantine would certainly provide other witnesses in Como and Milan, witnesses he'd have created, in fact, by changing that large banknote, by tipping generously in a café or one of any number of little tricks that had served to draw attention to him, leaving a memory of his person.

"So, you have nothing to tell me *about the fact itself*?"

"About the crime? About the author of the same? Certainly not."

"There remain, however, your powers of divination. You're a necromancer, aren't you?"

"I know a few divinatory practices: aeromancy, daphnomancy, lampadomancy, lecanomancy…"

Rapid knocking at the door interrupted his enumeration, which seemed like a joke.

"Who is it?" the inspector asked impatiently.

"Me," came Sani's voice.

De Vincenzi went to open the door.

"I must speak to you."

De Vincenzi went out into the corridor.

"Read this," and the deputy inspector held out a small, crumpled piece of paper.

Someone must have squashed it into a ball. Written in pencil in capital letters were the words:

THE FIRST: THE YOUNGEST, THE INNOCENT.
THIS ISN'T A WARNING.
IT'S THE BEGINNING OF A SERIES.

"Where did you find it?"

"In a corner of the first landing downstairs, close to the door that opens onto the stairs to the top floor. I was coming up to see you just now because I wanted to tell you several things, when that little white ball caught my eye. I picked it up and unfolded it. Do you think it's a joke?"

No, De Vincenzi did not think it was a joke.

"Have everyone come up to their rooms, lock themselves in and wait for me. I'll go to see each one in his or her own room myself. Go with them and then put the officers on guard in the corridor. You stay downstairs with the hotel managers. And keep an eye on the English couple in the parlour. Put Cruni on the top floor, but tell him to be on guard and not to hesitate to use his gun if necessary."

"What do you think is going on?"

"I don't know. I don't think anything."

He went back into the room and coldly ordered: "Novarreno, come to your room with me. I want to search your suitcases."

9

The search yielded nothing, of course. But there was something strange about Novarreno's room. What it was, De Vincenzi couldn't immediately say. Uncertainty was beginning to engulf him. The overcoat and hat of this trinkets-dealer—the one in thick, shaggy wool, saffron-yellow and impossible to forget, the other tiny and round, with a yellow and turquoise striped ribbon four fingers high—weren't they strange? Strange, too, the few books on black magic and the occult, Salomone's *Clavicole*, Collin de Plancy's *Dictionnaire Infernal* and Abbot Bianco's *Lessicomanzia*? The huge piece of rosin—strange? That violin without strings? Or the corked bottle with *Acqua amara* on its label? Everything and nothing was strange. It was the atmosphere. On the bed there was a scarlet travel rug as a blanket, in the glass on the nightstand an orchid. On the table, a pad of blue paper, a packet of envelopes and a bottle of ink. The suitcase with all the samples was on a chair in a corner.

"Would you like to see a few of my things?" He was ready to blow up the little pig, to make a shell bloom.

De Vincenzi stopped him. "Do you know if someone on this floor has a portable oil stove? Or an electric radiator?"

"Well, no—how should I know? The hotel has an oil stove that's kept in the one bathroom. They turn it on when someone wants to take a bath since the little room where they put the tub has no heating."

"So where is this bathroom?"

"At the end of the other part of the corridor; you go down some steps and the door is there. The stairway continues and leads to the billiard room."

Anyone could have taken the stove and carried it to Room 5 so the room would overheat and the body would lose its rigor mortis. But why? Just so they could take the body up to the top floor and hang it from a beam on the landing there? Always bearing in mind that the killer must have been sure no one would surprise him, and that he could act freely. Completely absurd. And yet… In that case, the window would have been opened afterwards in order to get rid of the smell of oil. A concatenation of circumstances, cleverly arranged but pointless, awkward and excessive, because the results of the killer's actions were obvious, so what was the point of trying to hide the clues? A waste of time and energy. It could be said that everything the killer had done in this crime had increased his difficulty and risks a hundredfold.

Novarreno fixed his small, penetrating black eyes on De Vincenzi. His vague smile could have been mocking—or challenging. Unless it masked some internal disturbance that was closer to fear…

"Does your clairvoyance reveal that, before dawn, there will be more than one body under the roof of this hotel?"

"You're joking." But his voice, normally warm, soft and melodious, was slightly sharp this time. Strident. Was he afraid of being killed himself?

"Which of these people did you know before meeting them here as guests of the hotel?"

"Not one of them."

But it wasn't true. De Vincenzi shrugged. He'd expected that

81

answer. He was looking for what it was that seemed strange in that room. All at once his face, which was furrowed and locked in mental concentration, relaxed and seemed to light up. He'd got it. In that room there were no letters, either on the table, in the drawers or anywhere else. There wasn't a trace of correspondence. Nor were there any pieces of paper with writing on them of any sort. Giorgio Novarreno, salesman, had taken care not to leave any trace whatsoever of his real business beyond that suitcase with its samples in his room. The room was at one and the same time occupied and empty. Everything it contained was for effect; it wasn't alive, and didn't reflect the life of the person who lived there. That was the odd thing. And the man's reticence, his lies… And the truths, too, which he thought useful to disclose… His occupation as a salesman— what actual work was it hiding?

"Don't leave this room. I'll come back to you."

"Can I go to bed?"

"If you wish."

De Vincenzi left the room and went into the corridor, closing the door behind him. Now he wanted to meet all the hotel guests, one after another. The killer was undoubtedly one of them. But would he manage to identify and expose him? Where to begin?

Sani was watching him from the landing. The officers were at their posts in the corridor. De Vincenzi stopped on the landing.

"Are the managers downstairs?"

"In the parlour."

"What about the guests who don't live at the hotel?"

"I've put them in the dining room—four in all, since according to the manager the others ran off in a hurry as soon as the hunchback announced what had happened, and before

82

Bianchi arrived. But the hotelier knows them all and they're easily traced."

"It won't be necessary."

He quickly went downstairs and into the parlour, throwing the door open suddenly. The woman was sitting where he'd left her, holding herself upright, stiff and staring ahead. At the sound of the door, Mrs Flemington immediately turned to look at the sofa in the opposite corner of the room. Mr Flemington appeared to be sleeping on it. The woman's large, glaucous eyes then moved towards the inspector; De Vincenzi read in them a desperate confusion. But the flash of terror disappeared immediately. Mrs Flemington was smiling now, yet her forced smile would not have fooled anyone. The woman was afraid. Who or what was frightening her so much? De Vincenzi looked at the sofa. Mr Flemington was lying across it, his head on the armrest and his feet on the ground. The fingers of his left hand, dangling over the floor, grasped a pipe. His eyes were closed and his breathing was heavy. The inspector's attention was drawn to a bottle and a glass on the table in the centre of the room; the whisky bottle was two-thirds empty. Who had brought it into this room? He remembered very well that he had not had it sent, though Flemington had asked for it. He had to believe that the Englishman had left the room or that someone had responded to his request. In any case, the couple had had some contact with the hotel manager or the waiter. So had the woman then learnt something more than he had told her in the first interview—and was that why she was so alarmed? Flemington had drunk enough alcohol to knock him out on that sofa.

"Are they going to give us a room at last? This hotel's way of treating us is very odd. Mr Flemington will put in a complaint tomorrow with our consul."

Of course. De Vincenzi knew it. Diplomatic objections and all the rest... The chief would be peeved with him, all the more so if nothing came out of this mess. Nothing? The killer. But what did these two English people so recently arrived in Milan have to do with anything?

"I wonder, Mrs Flemington, why your husband wouldn't listen to my advice about changing hotels?"

The woman glanced at the sofa again.

"Someone recommended this one to us... we have an itinerary. Mr Flemington has had his business correspondence sent here."

"What does Mr Flemington do?"

The woman pulled herself up and looked at De Vincenzi haughtily. "Flemington, of the firm Copthall and Flemington, solicitors to the Court, Lincoln's Inn Fields. My husband is one of the best-known lawyers in London."

De Vincenzi looked over at the snoring man, lips half open and pipe in his hand, the effects of whisky. But why would such a grand lawyer come to The Hotel of the Three Roses?

"Mrs Flemington, I speak your language, but not so well, I'd say, as to understand its subtleties. And you don't speak or understand Italian."

"So?"

Naturally, De Vincenzi was going the long way round. The woman, however, had immediately become suspicious and wanted to get to the point. She wanted to know right away, that much was clear. But what? What was she waiting for him to tell her?

"I'd like to be able to explain, in order to convince you."

"How?"

She was trembling with impatience. The man on the sofa moved and picked up the hand that was dangling. He was trying to turn round, to change position.

"Signora, there was a tragedy in this hotel some hours ago. A crime was committed, a horrible crime. A man was killed, a young man, and after his death he was strung up by his neck from a beam to make it seem as if he'd been hanged."

The woman, extremely pale, held her breath. She stared at De Vincenzi with glassy, glowing eyes, green as a cat's. Her pupils danced with hysteria and De Vincenzi saw, in their depths, convulsions of laughter, violent muscular contractions, the quick, clean punctures of a hypodermic needle on Pravaz's syringe. Such a sudden change would have terrified someone who'd tried to avoid provoking it, having seen it coming.

"Monstrous, isn't it?" He didn't wait for a reply. It wasn't forthcoming in any case. "And the young man who was killed, practically a boy, he was English, came from London. His name was—"

From behind him came a voice as dry, angry and sharp as a paper cut: "Douglas Layng."

This time it was as if De Vincenzi had been scorched by a red-hot iron. He turned round.

"How did *you* know?"

Flemington, the lawyer, was sitting up on the sofa. Although the whisky had gone to his legs, his brain was lucid. His sarcastic laugh was heard again.

"What do you think?"

"Nothing. But answer me: how did you know the dead man was called Douglas Layng?"

Flemington raised his hand with the diamond on it as if to placate De Vincenzi. "I came to Milan to this hotel in order to find Douglas Layng. *And I was afraid of arriving too late.* Unfortunately, my fear was justified. Is it really young Layng who's been killed?"

"It's him."

"How sad!" He stopped talking. His wife was crying, tears sliding silently down her cheeks and furrowing the layer of powder covering them.

Flemington slowly rose, and with small, perfectly regular steps went to stand beside his wife and put his hand on her shoulder.

"Diana," he said, and however tender he wished to sound, his voice conveyed an order rather than a tone of comfort.

"My wife held Douglas Layng on her lap as a baby." Removing his hand from her shoulder, he walked up to the inspector and with whisky-tinged breath said to his face, "Of course you must arrest the killer."

"Do you know him?"

"Bloody right! And it's crucial that he be arrested."

"What are you still afraid of?"

"Everything."

"Well, it will be easy to arrest him if you know who he is."

"Do you think so?" Once more his grating laugh could be heard like short hiccups. "It won't in fact be easy. I can tell you *who it was*, not *who it is now*. I have never met him in person. I couldn't point him out to you in order to shout: grab him! It will be necessary for you to discover who killed Douglas Layng. *Only then* will I be able to tell you why he was killed and why he was hung by the neck from a beam. And I will also be able to tell you the real name of the killer, who will of course have assumed another as of today."

De Vincenzi looked at him. Flemington now seemed in possession of all his faculties. What fantastical story did he have in store? Everything was fantastical, in any case. Everything that was happening. A nightmare.

"All doors to this hotel are being guarded," he murmured, just to say something. Because his thoughts were following an entirely different course.

The other man let out his peculiar, sharp laugh. The inspector's nerves were vibrating like the taut strings of a violin.

"Julius Lessinger habitually never went out through doors. It seems like a joke, right?" He turned to look at his wife, who had dried her eyes and recovered her stiff, upright dignity. He looked satisfied and rubbed his hands slowly. "My mission in coming here was to take young Layng back to London immediately. Now, there will be other catastrophes after this first one."

Even more than Flemington's words, the facts themselves made it seem as if young Layng had been killed by someone *who had begun methodically executing a criminal plan*, and the young man's murder was only the beginning. Who was the intended target?

"You spoke of catastrophes, Mr Flemington. Could you tell me what else you're worried about? And who is this Julius Lessinger you mentioned?"

"If the killer already knows about our arrival—and it's reasonably sure that he does—my wife and I are in danger." He said this perfectly calmly.

"In any case, the killer couldn't have known that you would be here last night, and it wasn't to give you a warm welcome that the body was set hanging on the top-floor landing."

The Englishman's eyes flashed. "The top floor, you say? Ah! just like down there! He took care of the details... until he could... Up there, right? Of course!"

But he wasn't laughing any more and his cheeks had turned somewhat blue. His wife sighed.

De Vincenzi stared at Flemington. "You don't want to tell me anything else, Mr Flemington?"

There was a brief hesitation before the man shook his head.

"No! Not yet…"

"Be careful. If not tonight, I shall be forced to make you speak tomorrow."

The other man shrugged. *"All in the course of twenty-four hours.* You'll need to hurry up, Inspector. Tomorrow I'll talk—if necessary."

"As you wish." And De Vincenzi turned round and headed for the door.

"Do we have to stay in this room? It's not the most comfortable place for a lady to spend the night."

"I'm sorry, but I have no choice. It's necessary that no one should see you for now, and in any case it's easier for me to keep you safe in here."

Flemington laughed again, but weakly. "You mean to say that you're putting a guard at the door?"

"And under that window, in the courtyard."

Flemington's laugh was once more sharp and sarcastic.

"Thank you, sir. This way, you can also be sure that we won't be going anywhere. But please have someone bring me some more whisky."

De Vincenzi left, closing the door behind him and turning the key in the lock.

Julius Lessinger… Either Flemington was lying, or he had revealed a name that definitely wasn't that of the killer. He'd said so himself.

10

Finding himself in the lobby again, De Vincenzi looked around. Where should he begin? With which of these twenty or more people? True, many of them—by reason of the nationality and personality of the murder victim—could definitely be eliminated. He said to himself, for one thing, that the crime could not have been committed by an Italian.

He took the list Bianchi had returned to him out of his pocket and reread the names: Vilfredo Engel, Carlo Da Como, Nicola Al Righetti, Carin Nolan, Stella Essington, Pompeo Besesti... Why had he put the name of Pompeo Besesti amongst the names of the suspects? Oh, yes: because he was the owner of the Bank of Pure Metals. And where was he from? Very rich, someone had said. It must have been Novarreno who'd told him. And the hunchback? Bardi, that perpetual busybody, knew a lot. It had of course been he who'd written the anonymous letter. But why? No. It wasn't possible to construct a hypothesis that would stand up, even a preposterous one. So he'd have to resign himself to questioning each person. Something would come out.

He walked to the dining room and entered it. Maria was sleeping, her blond head resting on her arms, which were folded over the desk. Mario, standing behind the counter, was awake, or almost, though his eyes were sleepy. And the two waiters, sitting in the corner, were dozing too. The four card-players were still engaged in their interminable match. Perhaps they were glad of the opportunity— however tragic—that gave them an excuse to stay at the table longer than usual. Seated next to the players, Virgilio and Captain Lontario seemed to be following the progress of the game, but in truth they were all straining towards the lobby and the voices issuing from it. The dining room was lit only in the corner where the group sat, because Virgilio had had the other lamps switched off.

De Vincenzi went straight to the hotel manager. "Have these people heard?"

Virgilio jumped to his feet so suddenly and awkwardly that the chair fell over behind him. The four put down their cards and stood up, facing the inspector. Lontario copied them, standing on his gammy leg with difficulty and leaning on his cane.

"War injury?" asked De Vincenzi.

"Yes," he responded with a sort of grunt. He wasn't pleased to be reminded of his infirmity, however glorious the cause.

"Have you known Signor Engel for long?"

"No. Why? I met him here."

"And why do you come to this place?"

"When we settled in Milan after the armistice, my mother and I, we lived in this hotel for a few months. Time enough to find an apartment and have our furniture sent from the Veneto, where we'd been living before that."

"So Signor Da Como, too?"

"All of them casual acquaintances."

"I see. But in any case, you've made actual friends of those two."

"If you want to call it friendship."

"What can you tell me about them?"

The captain laughed. "That they play piquet well— as they do many other games, for that matter..." He paused to stare at the inspector. "I don't believe I can be of any help to you, you know. I don't know a thing."

Verdulli, the theatre critic who was constitutionally green with bile, made his sharp voice heard.

"So the Englishman was hanged, eh? Just like in a novel by Poe!"

"Who are you?"

"Socrate Verdulli. Do you know me? I'm the editor of *Secolo*."

"And you?"

"Beltramo Pizzoni, of the Banca Commerciale."

"And you?"

"Me? I'm a painter. Igino Pico. Do you think I could see the body? I ran upstairs as soon as the hunchback raised the alarm, but I was sent downstairs immediately. I'd be interested to paint it. I'd light it from below, though, with a smoky candle..."

"You?" De Vincenzi turned to the last card-player and raised his voice to shut the painter up. Pico shook his head with pitiful distress. Taking his glass from the table, he drank its contents down in one gulp.

"I'm Giuliano Agresti from the *Gazzetta dello Sport*."

"Not one of you knows anything?"

What could they know?

"Fine. You can go on playing."

The four immediately sat down and picked up their cards.

"Now, who remembers which cards have been played?" Verdulli said ironically.

"May I go home?" the captain asked, and De Vincenzi nodded.

Lontario went straight to the coat rack at the back of the room, limping on his stiff leg.

"That one won't be coming back to the Three Roses!" Pico jested. He took Virgilio by the jacket and whispered in a comically grave voice: "Bring me another half-litre, kind Manager. We'll need a few to make it through to tomorrow."

De Vincenzi went towards the lobby. When he got to Maria's desk he noticed she was still sleeping, and took pity on her. He turned to her husband.

"Send your wife to bed. I'll question her tomorrow."

He left hurriedly. The first room he entered was Number 2, Stella Essington's. About thirty, Stella Essington, whose real name was the more common Rosa Carboni, pampered herself like a girl. Because she was waiting for the inspector, she'd put on pea-green pyjamas with yellow trim. Horrible things, enough to set the teeth on edge, like lemon juice. She was smoking, sucking on a long ivory holder encircled with pinkish diamonds.

"Make yourself at home, Inspector—I'll tell you everything I know—but not on that armchair; it wobbles." She offered him a soft chair.

De Vincenzi looked around. "Do you play the cello?"

She raised her hands to the heavens before his astonished face.

"Forgive me! If you only knew how the sound of the cello moves me! All my faculties vibrate like its strings."

She was leaning on the headboard and gently arching her back over it. Although she wasn't laughing, her lips were parted and drawn at the corners as in a rictus, and her pupils were shiny. She looked at the door, which De Vincenzi had left partly open, and frowned.

"We can be heard. Do you want to close it?"

"No one is listening."

"That's right. You'll have guards in the corridor. But what I have to tell you is very serious."

"What is it?"

"Only to you. On your word of honour as a gentleman. Ah! What a bore it is to talk like this!"

She moved away from the bed and stepped over to the mirror on the wardrobe. She regarded her figure and put a hand through her hair. All at once, as if severing an invisible bond, she headed for the nightstand beside the bed and made as if to open the drawer.

"No." The icy voice of De Vincenzi stopped her. "Not now. You must stop. And you must tell me who provides you with the drugs."

The response was immediate. The woman threw herself across the bed and began to sob; her shoulders, her entire body shook. De Vincenzi saw the yellow and green, and the unnatural red of her hair, cut short on a shaved neck and highlighted with brown. He shrugged. What could this one tell him? He started for the door. He would lock the woman in her room. But Stella Essington heard his steps and bounced up like a spring. She turned to him, again raising her hands towards the ceiling.

"No! Holy Virgin! You must hear me out! I beg you, listen to me," she screamed.

"Don't scream, for—" and he forced himself to stop, in order not to swear. Who had advised him to begin with her? "Don't scream, or I'll go."

"OK, but listen to me." She looked around for her ivory cigarette-holder, which had fallen on the bed, and lit another cigarette, taking it out of her pyjama pocket along with a box of matches. "That poor boy… Oh! it's terrible!" She put her face in her hands. "Oh! If I could only calm my nerves! I had to contain myself for so long down there in the dining room, where you penned us up like beasts." She turned hastily and pointed melodramatically to the bed. "I'll die in that bed. I feel it."

"Tell me instead: where did he die—that young man?"

"How do you know he didn't die by hanging?" Her eyes sparkled maliciously.

"Don't worry about that. But I don't know where he was killed and I'm waiting for you to tell me."

"I… He was very friendly with me. Me alone, amongst all the ladies in this hotel. Have you seen them? Pah! They're worthless. The only one whose friendship meant anything to him was me. He used to say he wanted to take me to England…"

"What else did he say to you?" He went over to her and lowered his voice to a whisper. "Do you know why he was killed?"

He waited. She was, perhaps, talking nonsense. But maybe it was better to let her speak.

"He was killed because he was going to inherit a million pounds. It's true! Don't you believe me?"

A million pounds. The whole of Rosa Carboni was summed up in that fantastic figure. But apart from the sum, what did she really know, this woman? "Get the hunchback to tell you. He knows a lot. He lies like a slut when he talks about people who know how to keep him at the requisite distance, who aren't of his class. He's always hated me, he has! I don't respect him anyway. But if he wanted to tell everything he knew…"

"Good. I'll speak to Signor Bardi. Now go to bed and stay calm. Tomorrow morning we'll talk everything over."

He hesitated. Should he turn out her stash next to the bed? Ether, or cocaine—there was always the risk of finding the woman the worse for wear the next morning. But he shrugged.

If he started seizing drugs, it would raise the alarm in the hotel, and the important thing at the moment was to move quickly. If Julius Lessinger really...

"Did he confide anything in you, the young Englishman?"

"Why?"

"Did he mention anyone in particular?"

"Why?"

She was on the defensive. She threw a glance at the nightstand.

"Go to the devil!" De Vincenzi said to himself. He left and locked the door.

One down. Who next? Number 3 was staring him in the face—in black, on the door. He looked at the hotel plan he'd put in his pocket. That door opened onto the room of Pompeo Besesti, the director of the Bank of Pure Metals. He hesitated. He'd need to use tact with this one. The chief's words rang in his ears, those he'd let fall as he'd touched the flower on his lapel. *You have no relationships with any of these people. I prefer it that way. You'll have free rein. Are you with me?...* He lifted the latch and opened the door. The room was dark. Could it be that he was sleeping?

"That room is empty, sir." It was the officer on guard at the bend in the corridor.

Empty? He turned on the lights. Bed remade. A gleam on the silver toiletry items. A chest. In the middle of the room— how large that room was! At least six by eight metres—a table at the foot of the bed, with many cards and several logbooks on it. He saw some yellow bars under the leather blotter. He picked them up. He was no expert, but he guessed they must be gold. They were stamped: 20K. Pure gold. One was green. So he left them lying around like that. But why was he not back at three in the morning? De Vincenzi went into the corridor and called Sani.

"Phone headquarters. Franceschi must be on duty. Tell him to send a few good officers from the flying squad to do the rounds of the local bars. I want them to catch Pompeo Besesti, but not arrest him, and when they find him—if they find him—keep him dangling without letting him know why, and find out where he was from eight yesterday evening till now."

"But—"

"Be quick about it!"

Sani went downstairs. The telephone was in the lobby near the toilets.

Why, though, did it seem strange to De Vincenzi that Pompeo Besesti wasn't in his own room at three in the morning? He closed and locked that door too. The first room he came to round the corner of the corridor was Number 12: Mary Alton Vendramini, the widow who'd arrived from England that day. But everyone was arriving from England! And yet, this one…

He knocked softly and before she could respond he opened the door and closed it behind him. Slowly he turned. Only his tiredness and the unconscious need to proceed quickly with this new encounter had induced him to enter the room in that way. He was also lost in an insoluble problem and troubled by the whirl of his feelings.

What he saw inside the room made him jump. Lying on a rug in the middle of the room, Mary Alton Vendramini was looking at a porcelain doll clothed in a rosy gauze dress, her arms reaching out for a hug. Such was De Vincenzi's amazement that he was rendered speechless for several minutes. Another doll… With each step he took in the investigation, he found unexpected connections between all these people when it seemed there shouldn't be any. And this one here had arrived only this morning.

The woman—now that she had taken off her hat and veil—looked truly beautiful. A pure profile, a small head of golden-blond hair. Her heavy plait was wound from the base of her neck to her crown. Her thin eyebrows were arched and her strangely violet irises were dark behind extremely long eyelashes. Passionate lips on a perfect mouth. Her body was thin, yet full and soft under a clingy black silk dress. Her legs, sheathed in the shiny black material, could be seen under a short knee-length petticoat. She was lying on her side, with her legs folded under her.

She raised her head and took a long, sad look at De Vincenzi, who'd stayed next to the closed door. Taking the doll in her arms, she made as if to get up. Almost unconscious of what he was saying, De Vincenzi murmured, "Don't trouble yourself." But he immediately recovered his coldness and asked brusquely, "Who gave you that doll?"

"Why do you ask that?" the woman replied. She was standing in front of him. "It's mine!"

She squeezed the doll ever closer to her breast, as if she feared he would take it from her.

11

He must not let the allure of her sweet, sad beauty get the better of him, De Vincenzi commanded himself. Since he was still young then, almost a novice—the horrifying crime with which he was concerned was his first important case—his reaction was inevitably strong, and the tone of his questions strained.

"Tell me the story of this doll."

"Why do you believe there's a story to it?"

Mary Alton Vendramini answered quietly, her voice sweet and full of childish notes. There was great candour in her and in her violet eyes, so deep and velvety.

"Your husband is an officer in the English army?"

"He was. He died two weeks ago."

"Why did you come to Italy?"

"Because I'm Italian."

"Do you have family in Milan?"

"No. My family has nothing more to do with me. I haven't come back for my family!"

"Did you know Douglas Layng?"

The woman stared at De Vincenzi without speaking.

"Answer me."

"I did not know him."

"*Why*, then, did you come to this hotel and *why did you arrive this very day*?"

She trembled. "I'm cold," she murmured. Holding crossed arms with long, white, diaphanous hands, she shivered, squeezing the doll ever more tightly against her breast.

De Vincenzi noted that Room 12 was small, and filled almost entirely by the large double bed. It was overheated. He was sweating.

"Signora, the crime committed against that young man is one of the most atrocious imaginable!"

"I've been here alone since yesterday morning."

At the foot of the bed was an armchair. The woman—so tiny, fragile and blonde—fell into it. Her legs sparkled under the transparent silk covering them. She continued to look at him, but he couldn't get a handle on her. De Vincenzi had to struggle to overcome a sort of vertigo. For more than three hours he'd been exhausting his brain power in the delicate game of seeking the end of a thread to guide him. He was worn out, exasperated. Anyone he'd interrogated could have given him that thread, and instead they were all hiding it. Novarreno, Bardi, the hunchback, Flemington and his wife... and now this one here. What had he found out by now? Nothing! A doll on an iron bed—on the top floor—in the dark—and now another, similar doll in the arms of this woman who was hiding behind her innocence in order not to say anything. Nothing at all. Or was it the same doll? Absurd! Cruni was on guard upstairs. No one could have gone up there. He grabbed a chair and practically threw it onto the floor in front of the armchair. He sat down.

"Look, Signora, we cannot go on like this! Tell me why you came to this hotel. Why you have a doll like that one there... Tell me how you are linked to the tragedy that's taken place here, that's still unfolding..." He was answered by silence. "It isn't possible for you to keep silent. Sooner or later, I will know why. No one is leaving here until I find out." Silence. He looked resigned. "You must answer me, Signora. I'm prepared to go on with my questioning for hours, until you are exhausted by the very sound of my voice. Tell me about your husband. He died two weeks ago, you tell me. Where?"

"In Sydney."

"Of what illness?"

"He was old, my husband, and he'd had an adventurous life in the colonies. A hard life."

"Where?"

"South Africa."

"Where did you meet him?"

A smile. "What do you know about me?"

"Nothing. But don't delude yourself. By tomorrow I'll know everything. It's pointless lying or keeping quiet. I'll find out everything about you."

"I know it's pointless. However... You think I don't wish to speak because I have something to hide, something compromising. Something a person can't confess, is that right?"

"I don't think anything. Answer me."

She shook her golden head. "No, no, it's not that. *I'm afraid.* I can't speak!" Her voice remained quiet and low, but she wasn't lying. She was afraid. Like Novarreno, like Bardi the hunchback, like Mrs Flemington, like the lawyer Flemington—underneath his posturing and aggressive sarcasm.

Of what? And of whom?

"Do you know Julius Lessinger?"

She jumped to her feet. She'd gone so white as to look nearly blue. Thus bloodless, her features appeared even more delicate, evanescent, indistinct. But she didn't waver. De Vincenzi didn't feel the need to reach out, for fear that she'd fall. She was afraid

100

but she wouldn't faint. She was pale, but her violet eyes were as dark as a stormy sky.

"Who told you about… about him?"

She realized she was still holding the porcelain doll, which was completely pink, too pink, with those rosettes flaming high on both cheeks. She went to the chest of drawers—one step and she was there, so small was the room—and put it down. The doll lay with its hands in the air and its legs askew. Mary then turned round and sat down in the armchair. She pulled her petticoat over her knees and sat with her feet together, composed, almost rigid. Her chest heaved a little, beating against the snug silk of her dress.

"I'll tell you what I know. In the meantime—" she shook her head, forlorn and discouraged—"fate!"

"Did you really arrive in Milan this morning?"

"There's a stamp from border control on my passport. You can check it. This morning… *In any case, it was for tomorrow only.*"

"What was?"

"Right, you don't know! No one has told you."

"Which of those in this hotel could have told me?"

"You'll meet them."

"Who? Give me their names."

"Their names? How many? I don't know. It's the truth—I don't know. Everyone who has an interest in hearing Major Harry Alton's will."

"And you, his widow…"

"Yes, me. His widow, however, will perhaps be the only one not to inherit."

"Go ahead. Tell me." De Vincenzi was feeling impatient. By now, he was afraid himself. He had the impression that every minute lost could make this tragedy worse.

"My husband is dead. He'd turned seventy-four... When he went to the Cape, which was then Transvaal and Orange, he was under thirty. That was 1880." She paused.

"And?"

"I don't know... don't know. I'm ignorant of everything that happened down there. I know that Harry went there fairly poor. He had his army pay, and it was then that he started his career." She wrung her hands. "When he died in Sydney—two weeks ago—he left a legacy of five or six hundred thousand pounds."

"And Douglas Layng?"

"Not yet, not yet! Yes, Douglas Layng... but don't rush things." She stopped. "Why did you mention Julius Lessinger? Is he really in Milan too?" She bowed her head, talking to herself: "And who'd have killed Douglas Layng like that if not him?"

"Do you know Julius Lessinger?"

"Know him? No. I know his reputation—it's unspeakable. But what did he do to earn it? Not one of those who fear him today knows him any more. Julius Lessinger was with my husband in Transvaal as one of his soldiers."

"Just a moment," growled De Vincenzi. He got up and stared at her, his voice clipped: "Who was down there in Transvaal with your husband?" He held his breath for her reply. Whom would she name?

The woman felt the gravity of his question, and the importance of her reply. Her pallor, if anything, had increased. Slowly she said: "Major Alton commanded a light battalion. He had two officers with him."

"Names!" hissed De Vincenzi.

"—William Engel—"

He was not startled, but asked in an icy voice, "How is that possible? A German?"

"An Englishman of German origin."

"Go on!"

"—Dick Nolan—"

"Who else?"

"The soldiers… a hundred or so, and Julius Lessinger was one of them."

"Fine," said De Vincenzi, suddenly calm. He sat down again. He was tranquil now. "Go on."

Mary paused for some time. When she began to speak again, it seemed as if she were reciting a lesson—or, more likely, recounting a fable. Even her voice was the same: monotonous.

"The Vaal crocodiles, between Kimberley and Johannesburg…" She raised her violet eyes to De Vincenzi, as if expecting him to interrupt. But the inspector did not speak. "It's a story about crocodiles!"

"Go on."

The woman slowly rose. She went to the corner where she'd put her suitcase on a small table. She looked around for the key, rummaging in the drawers of the dresser, and found it in her handbag inside the wardrobe. She opened the suitcase. Silk, see-through linens. Soft colours. A silver box, the silver tops of bottles kept in place against the lid with leather straps… She took out a letter from under folded linens. The oversized envelope bore franked blue and red stamps; on the back, a large impression in black sealing wax. She held it out to the inspector.

De Vincenzi read the woman's name and London address. He looked at the postmark: Sydney.

"Read it," and she fell back into the armchair.

The letter was typewritten—in English, of course—on a large sheet of heavy paper which bore the signature of Harry

Alton. A military man's signature—large, firm, with rounded, exaggerated capital letters and a great flourish on the N of Alton. *My little Mary…* Yet after that affectionate phrase, the tone changed and became terse, almost angry.

> My little Mary,
>
> There's no further need for you to consider joining me in Australia. I'm about to leave. It's true! The doctor, whom I ordered not to lie to me, has given me one or two months to live at most. In any case, my ongoing suffering is such that I will cut things short myself. I'm writing to the lawyer, Flemington, to give him all the information necessary to look after things when I'm gone. He'll invite you and a few others somehow linked to my fate to gather in Milan in a certain hotel I have specified and which Flemington in any case knows. There you'll learn your destiny; by which I mean the financial destinies that await you.
>
> I have nothing against you. In the five years during which you've been my wife, I have had to recognize in you the great virtue of adaptability. You accepted the hand of an old man for personal profit, but you have loyally maintained our agreement. I, for my part, intend to maintain my family, and I'm taking every precaution so that someone I know does not frustrate my wishes after my death.
>
> Don't be surprised at the journey you must make or the people you'll meet in Milan. It's necessary for everyone to convene in that city and in that hotel.
>
> I don't want to tell you anything else. Anyway, life's only interest is in the surprises it has in store for us, and I have reserved one for you that's not the least bit banal. When you learn the other, less edifying details of the life of

old Harry, you'll just say that all men are swine, fighting
each other to get their snouts in the trough.

This was followed by his signature and a postscript written in pen:

You must take the porcelain doll with you on your journey.

De Vincenzi sat holding the sheet of paper for several moments. The woman raised her head to look at him. An unhealthy fear continued to preoccupy her, and it was exhausting her. The inspector looked at the porcelain doll on the dresser.

"How does Julius Lessinger come into this?"

"I know nothing, or very little about Harry's life. I know only that Julius Lessinger was a soldier with him down there in 1900, during the Boer War, and that afterwards Major Alton was afraid of him."

"Flemington was the major's lawyer?"

"Yes, but more than that, a friend. They shared many interests."

"And some inadmissible secret?"

"I don't know."

"Did Flemington also fear Lessinger?"

"How did you know?"

"Flemington is in Milan, in this hotel."

"Oh! Then—" But she stopped herself.

"Well?"

The woman shrank still further into the chair, shaken with trembling, which couldn't have been from the cold.

"And?"

"And now Douglas Layng is dead!"

"Are you saying that things are going differently from the way your husband intended?"

"Flemington will know."

"Who was Layng? How did he figure in this story—which seems as if it's been going on for years—the poor kid? He'd hardly begun to live!"

"Flemington must know."

"And you?"

"No."

"How long ago did your husband leave for Australia? Why didn't he take you with him?"

"The major left a year ago. He had a lot of business there." Her reply was vague and reticent.

"Was he facing some danger in England?"

"The lawyer, Flemington, will be able to tell you."

"Was it because of this danger that he went on his own, leaving you behind in London?"

"What more can I tell you? I don't know—I don't know anything either. I've tried to understand, to find out. But why go on now? Five days ago Flemington gave me notice to leave for Italy, to come to this hotel and wait for his arrival. The meeting with all the people Major Alton mentioned will take place on 6 December, or so the lawyer told me."

"Today."

"Yes."

De Vincenzi looked at his watch. It was about four in the morning, and he'd told himself he'd solve the puzzle before dawn.

"Did you know that a doll just like this one is in the possession of a man in this hotel? A man called Vilfredo Engel?"

She opened her eyes and batted her eyelashes. "No."

"Do you know Vilfredo Engel?"

"No."

"And yet you know that one of your husband's officers had that name."

"William Engel, yes. But I never met him."

"You say he's English?"

"I believe he is."

"Tell me the story of your porcelain doll."

"My husband had it when he married me."

"Since we're on the subject, how did you meet Major Harry Alton?"

"It was in London, in 1914. I was dancing in a music hall."

De Vincenzi looked at the woman, who now more than ever had an air of ethereal innocence and fragility. How different she was from Stella Essington. Perhaps more dangerous, however. In any case, she had succeeded in marrying a major. Tomorrow she would be inheriting five or six hundred thousand pounds. Would she, though? What the devil could be the meaning of this meeting in Milan at The Hotel of the Three Roses? Would the reading of the will contain some surprises for her as well as for the others gathered here? Who were the others? Layng—who'd been killed, probably to get him out of the way... And then there was Nolan, Carin Nolan, maybe the daughter of the officer who'd fought with Alton in the Transvaal... And then there was Vilfredo Engel. How close a relation was that burly, panting piquet player, friend of Carlo Da Como, to the officer William Engel?

De Vincenzi knew he'd made great progress since he'd entered Room 12, but there was plenty more for him to do, and even when he'd managed to understand the details of this fantastical, knotty story he'd still be a long way from arresting the killer. Unless… unless it was true that the series had just begun and the killer would find it necessary to give another terrible sign of his presence.

"So that's how you married Harry Alton."

"It was he who asked me, insisting on his terms. I hadn't hidden anything about my past from him."

"Did you know the major was rich?"

"Your question is at the very least discourteous, Inspector. But I will answer you. My life had not been happy. If I was reduced to dancing in music halls and touring the cities of Europe and America—"

"You've been in America?"

"Yes."

"Where? Which cities?"

There was an almost imperceptible hesitation, but it didn't escape De Vincenzi.

"Several. New York for sure… and… and others. I was telling you that I did not like the life I had to lead. Yet I wouldn't have wanted to live miserably with my parents in Italy, either. That's why I left home. But in London, Paris… New York… and other places…" She shivered, almost twitched in the armchair. All at once she got up. "Well, when Major Alton offered his hand in marriage, I accepted, because I knew he was rich and that life with him would be easy and calm. There you have it!"

"And now?" De Vincenzi asked ruthlessly, although he knew that Signora Alton's cynicism was above all the result of the tense situation in which she found herself.

But he couldn't wait for her reply. Quick steps could be heard in the corridor and Sani was shouting loudly, "Where is the inspector?" He didn't have time to get to the door before Sani appeared at it, followed by the officers.

"What's going on?"

"I was in the lobby downstairs when I heard a thud overhead, like that of a body falling. The noise seemed to come from one of the first rooms near the garden, Number 5 or 6."

"Let's go," De Vincenzi said laconically. He turned to the widow as he was leaving. "Get some rest, Signora. I'll come back to you tomorrow. You haven't told me the story of your doll yet."

12

"Where were you?"

The officer pointed to the corner where both parts of the corridor met: the longer one, where Room 12 was the first room—and where De Vincenzi had been with Mary Alton—and the other, which aligned with the landing and on which Rooms 5, 6 and 7 opened, across from Rooms 1 to 4. The first part of the corridor was very long and ended on the left with the small stairway that led downstairs to the billiard room.

"Actually in that corner, were you? Were you watching both parts of the corridor?"

The man seemed to want to make excuses.

"I walked down this corridor, right to the end."

"So the lobby and the other corridor were left unguarded?"

"What could I do? I knew the stairs and the lobby were being watched. And you were in there. I thought—"

"Fine! Go back down to the end now." The doors on the first part of the corridor were all closed. De Vincenzi headed straight for that of Room 5 and opened it: the room where Douglas Layng had been living was empty, the bed made, the dresser drawer—the one in which Sani had found the packet of letters tied with ribbon—still partly open. "Take the letters out of that drawer. You can give them to me later. I want to read them."

Those letters now interested him. Sani hurried to obey and the packet of letters with English postmarks disappeared into his pocket. They left the room. De Vincenzi went up to the door of Novarreno's room.

Absolute silence.

"Novarreno," he called out. "Open up!"

No reply. He lifted the latch, but the door wouldn't open. It was locked from the inside. After several more tries, De Vincenzi waited no longer. He took two steps backward and threw his shoulder against the right-hand side. It offered no resistance and broke open.

The light was on in the room and the trinkets-salesman lay on the ground, a dagger plunged into the middle of his chest. De Vincenzi bent down a moment to look at him. He touched his hand: it was still warm, but he was surely dead. He leapt over the body and ran to the window, which was wide open. He leant out to look at the garden. Down below, on the ground floor, he saw a lit window: it had to be the one in the blue room, where he'd left Flemington and his wife. He turned to Sani, who'd come into the room and was looking at the body, horrified, while the officers stood at the door.

"You didn't put an officer on guard in the garden outside the parlour window as I ordered you to do?"

Sani was shaken. "I didn't have the heart to send a man out to stand in the rain. There's no way of leaving the garden apart from through the glass door which leads to the lobby, and I was in the lobby with two officers. After all, the door at the back of the building is also being watched."

De Vincenzi limited himself to giving Sani a look of disapproval. "This poor man wouldn't be dead if you'd followed my orders." He turned to the officers. "Phone the emergency medical service and the doctor." He went back to the window. The killer had entered and left through it, there could be no

111

doubt, as evidenced by the door locked on the inside. "Give me a torch."

Sani offered his own. De Vincenzi tried to see outside. As he had guessed, there was a ladder at the base of the wall. The killer had used it to go up and down and then he'd laid it on the ground against the wall. He'd gone to some trouble even in this, given how easy it had been for him to carry out the rest. And the ladder on the ground showed that the man no longer needed it, after the murder, to climb up to his own room, which clearly had to be on the ground floor. There were no windows on the garden other than the window of the blue room, still lit up, and the two kitchen windows across from it. The kitchen led directly into the dining room.

The rain continued falling insistently. The garden was flooded. He certainly wouldn't find any footprints there. Footprints, no; but whoever had carried out that acrobatic enterprise must have been soaking, and certainly, once out of the rain, would have left wet prints wherever he'd walked. De Vincenzi stepped over the body once more, almost running past Sani and the other officers as he threw himself down the large stairway. He moved the officer on guard aside and opened the door to the parlour. Flemington, his elbows on the table and his head in his hands, was staring at the glass in front of him. A short distance from the glass was the empty whisky bottle. The lawyer had removed his jacket, collar and tie. Mrs Flemington was sleeping on the sofa.

At the sound of the door opening, Flemington stirred from his contemplation and looked at the inspector without the least surprise. Suddenly his eyes flashed with terror, as if he'd only just recognized him. But his voice was mocking: "Still awake, Inspector. Wretched night, this!" And he let out his peculiar laugh. But it was only a brief acknowledgement. His face immediately darkened and beneath his bushy eyebrows his grey eyes clouded over.

De Vincenzi looked at the closed window, the floor. Not a trace.

"There's another dead man here, Mr Flemington."

"Oh," said the man. *"All in the space of twenty-four hours!* I told you so."

"We'll be speaking at length before long, Mr Flemington. I've come now just to—"

"—to see if I needed anything." That hiccuping, sarcastic laugh. "No! I don't need a thing."

"You don't want to ask me who's dead?"

He hunched his shoulders and got up slowly, propping himself against the table. Standing, he seemed heavy, if not enormous; with that bulk, how could he have got over the windowsill, seized the ladder and climbed up to the window? And then—having arrived at the hotel a few hours ago, only to be locked in that room—how could he have known which window was Novarreno's? And besides, why Novarreno?

"Mr Flemington, how many people have been asked to convene in this hotel to hear the reading of Major Harry Alton's will?"

"Have you heard? Five, and young Layng was one of them, though he is no more."

"One of these people is called—was called—Giorgio Novarreno?"

Flemington looked at him with profound, unfeigned surprise.

"What did you say?"

"Giorgio Novarreno, a Levantine."

"No. Why ever… Is he the dead man you mentioned?"

"Yes."

"I don't understand."

He didn't, in fact, understand. He was lost in thought, in intense reflection. The dead man clearly didn't come into it.

"That's fine, Mr Flemington. I'll come back in a bit. Meanwhile, give some thought to the benefit—to you as well as me—of deciding to tell me everything you know."

So Novarreno had nothing to do with the inheritance business, the dolls or with the lawyer, Flemington, of the firm Copthall and Flemington, Lincoln's Inn Fields. Unless he was Julius Lessinger… De Vincenzi shrugged his shoulders dramatically. Impossible! Not at his age; Novarreno couldn't be more than forty. So why had someone killed him? And now that he had to dismiss the possibility that Flemington had killed him, who was left? The killer had come in through the window, no doubt about it. So: someone had to have come from the kitchen or another room with windows looking out on the garden.

He walked without stopping past the open door of Room 6, where Sani and the two officers were with the body, and made his way slowly down the corridor, looking at the doors on the left. He consulted the guest list and the hotel plan provided by the owner. Nicola Al Righetti was in Room 7; in Room 8, Vittoria Jumeta Zogheb; in 9, Carin Nolan; in 10, Donato Desatta. Room 11 was empty.

But then how could the person who'd delivered the fatal blow have got down to the garden and gone up to the chiromancer's room when the ladder was now lying on the ground? Or was he dealing with an acrobat agile enough to get down to the garden and then back up without the help of the ladder?

However it had happened, whom should he suspect amongst all those whose rooms were on that part of the corridor? Two men: Nicola Al Righetti and Donato Desatta. He'd already questioned Al Righetti and Donato Desatta was the owner of the Orfeo, a bar in the centre with drinking and dancing until four in the morning.

He slowly retraced his steps. He stopped for a moment in front of Room 10 before proceeding. He was going to eliminate Desatta from the investigation, because he still believed the crime could not have been committed by an Italian. The same hand, perhaps the same knife had killed both young Layng and Giorgio Novarreno; and Douglas Layng had been hung from a rope in a macabre manner, on the top-floor landing, many hours after he'd been killed. Besides, De Vincenzi knew Desatta. He'd seen him moving between rooms at the Orfeo. He was a man of over fifty who tried desperately to avoid going bald by using dyes and cosmetics on his sparse, mousy-blond hair, and also to maintain a trim physique. A fun-loving, jovial man. De Vincenzi couldn't imagine him plotting all that or carrying out such a diabolical scheme. Nicola Al Righetti was the only one left: the man with the alibis who didn't want to be woken from a deep sleep…

He looked at the two doors in the corner: that of Room 7 on the first side and 9 on the longer side. In the first one was the American; in the second, Carin Nolan, a Norwegian about nineteen years old—"the threatened innocent", as Sani had ironically put it. In any event, she had to be the daughter or a relative of Officer Nolan who'd been in South Africa with Major Alton. What the devil had they done in the Transvaal, those three: Alton, Engel and Nolan? And why was Carin Norwegian? Perhaps her father was something of a soldier of fortune, like William Engel, who was originally from Germany? The Transvaal… diamond mines… Julius Lessinger, who'd turned up after twenty years in order to revenge himself or take control of the rich spoils. Someone everyone was afraid of, starting with the sarcastic, hiccuping Flemington, who drank whisky like water.

Lost in thought, De Vincenzi stared at the doors of the rooms, the corridor, the lobby. The officers stood stationary at the door of Novarreno's room, where the body lay stretched out on the floor. And Cruni was on the third-floor landing, guarding the other dead man whose heart had been stabbed many hours ago… Mary Alton Vendramini was playing with her doll… Stella Essington would be stupefied with heroin or cocaine… And she wanted to hear the cello played, to soothe the feverish agitation of her nerves… He shook himself and went towards Room 6. Sani came up to him.

"There was no struggle. To the naked eye it seems he didn't even leave prints."

What prints could he have left? De Vincenzi studied the body. Novarreno was still dressed as he had been when he'd left him a few hours earlier. "Go to bed," he'd told him, "if you want." But the Levantine hadn't done so. Tall, thin, with that sharp profile of his—no flesh on his face, just skin and bones—he seemed like a great bird of prey shot down in flight, eyes wide open, glassy and full of terrified astonishment. No, there'd been no struggle. The very fact that Novarreno had let his eventual killer enter his room through the window meant he must have known him. *A man was killed in this room, at precisely 12.30 yesterday. There is still a lot of blood in here…* How had he known? It was surely true, what he'd said, and for that knowledge he'd paid with his life. A shady character, in any

116

case. He knew everything, or nearly everything, but he hadn't talked. After his first sentence, uttered more as a stunt, to make an impression, *in order to act the necromancer,* Novarreno had retreated behind a wall of reticence, his alibis well prepared, determined to say only what could serve him. What had he been turning around in that tortured brain of his, so clever at preparing tricks? But he was also uncomplicated. He was plotting blackmail. In possession of a terrible secret, he must have known its worth in gold. And he'd been killed so that someone did not have to pay him—to shut him up.

"Cover his face with a hand towel," he ordered Sani brusquely.

De Vincenzi turned his back on the body. It had to be like that. Novarreno had wanted to join this atrocious game and he'd been fleeced. The circle was closing in. *All in the span of twenty-four hours.* Would he be able to put a stop to the series of murders, given that the dead man here was not part of it but an unforeseen *accident*? He'd have to hurry and couldn't afford to take one false step. His adversary was the sort who never misses a chance, and never loses.

"When will the doctor be here? Have him give me the knife."

"Did you look at it? It's a switchblade, but it must have an extremely thin blade."

"I'll look at it later."

There was time. If the killer had left it in the wound, De Vincenzi couldn't hope that it would furnish any clues, and as for fingerprints, one no longer finds them, not even in detective stories.

The hotel doorbell rang, as long, loud and insistent as a blowtorch. The inspector went down a few steps and leant over the balustrade. An officer had leapt out of the wicker chair

117

he'd been sleeping in and was proceeding towards the door. Virgilio appeared, sleepy, and staggered towards the door of the dining room.

A rather ostentatious man entered the hotel, with a blond beard, a fur coat with a mink collar and a brand-new grey hat on his head. He was smiling, showing off a set of bright white teeth. He twirled a stick with a gold knob.

"Good evening, Signor Besesti."

"You might wish me a good morning instead, my dear Virgilio." He was wary. "Have you put on a night guard?" and he pointed behind him to the officer, who was walking around.

He started going upstairs. On the landing he came face to face with De Vincenzi.

"Signor Pompeo Besesti?"

He was so surprised his monocle fell out of his eye.

"What's wrong?"

"I'm from the police."

The other man laughed. "Very pleased to meet you." But he wavered for a moment before regaining his composure. "I don't understand."

"I don't believe there's anything that directly concerns you, but I'd ask you to agree to a short interview."

"At this hour?" He raised his shoulders, faintly condescending. "Would you like to come to my room?" and he went on without waiting for De Vincenzi's consent.

De Vincenzi quickly moved in front of him and closed the door to Room 6 so he wouldn't see the body. Then he turned and waited for Besesti to enter his room first, a room that more or less faced Novarreno's. When Besesti put out his hand to turn the doorknob, a slight tremor made him lose his grip. The door wouldn't open.

"I forgot my key."

"Here it is."

As he took it, the director of the Bank of Pure Metals furrowed his brow and pursed his lips.

13

They remained standing, one on each side of the table with the yellow, white and green gold ingots on it. De Vincenzi saw the huge diamond sparkling on the other man's chest, and his crystal-clear blue eyes also sent out dark flashes. He felt Besesti was ready for a fight. What was he afraid of?

"How long have you been in Milan, Signor Besesti?"

"About two months."

"Where are you from?"

"South America."

"Are you Italian?"

"Originally, as my name would imply. I was born in Argentina."

"Have you ever been to South Africa?"

"No, never."

It seemed to De Vincenzi that his reply came a bit too quickly.

"Or the United States?"

"No."

"England?"

"Are you planning to say a rosary of the world, asking me if I've been in every country?"

"Not all of them, but I would like to hear your reply to my question about England."

"Do you intend to tell me why you're asking me these questions?"

De Vincenzi smiled. However exhausted he was from lack of sleep and nervous tension, this interview amused him. He couldn't have said why even to himself. What could he have against this rich man who was, one would suppose, used to giving orders and respected by everyone? His very wealth excluded him from suspicion of having committed such a crime. But was it a crime *for gain*, this one? The inspector reached out and toyed with one of the precious gold bars.

"You seem not to be worried about leaving these gold bars around."

The blue eyes looked at the gold ingots.

"Those are samples. I was hoping to deliver them to someone who lives in this hotel, to give him some work."

"Carlo Da Como?"

"Exactly! How did you know?"

"Have you known Signor Da Como for long?"

The reply came after a short pause.

"I met him in Milan."

"Or in London?"

"Why London?"

"Have you been to London, yes or no?"

"Of course I've been there. But what possible interest can you have in knowing that?"

"Did you ever meet Major Harry Alton?"

This time Pompeo Besesti paled visibly.

"I met him by chance. Not in London, however."

"Where were you yesterday afternoon and evening, and last night until four this morning?"

"Well, honestly, will you explain to me first what reason and what right you have to ask me all these questions?"

"A crime was committed in this hotel yesterday."

"What do you think I have to do with this crime of yours?"

"Douglas Layng was stabbed in the back."

"No!" It was a cry of anguish. But he recovered himself. "Did someone kill that young man?" His eyes were brimming with sadness—and also with terror. "But why? Why him of all people?"

"Well, he wasn't the only one to be killed," the icy voice of the inspector continued.

It was a rapid transformation: Pompeo Besesti lost all his triumphant self-assurance. His eyes shone dully, as if the light in them had been extinguished. His cheeks sagged, and the slight tremor that had barely been noticeable before was now almost a convulsion. It was startling.

"Do you wish to sit down?" De Vincenzi asked kindly.

Besesti practically brushed him away.

"Why do you want me to sit down!" Even his voice was no longer his own; its full, round sonority was broken and it became weak and shrill. He went on. "All right, tell me everything. It's necessary for me—and for you. And I'll tell you what sort of ties linked me—" But he stopped himself and looked the other man in the face with severity. "In any case, it could be that what I know has nothing to do with the boy's death, and what I know may be of no interest to the Italian police. Who killed him?"

A moment earlier, De Vincenzi had been feeling some pity for Besesti and would have saved him, tried to conduct the interview with some delicacy. But with the sudden return of fire in this insolent, vulgar man, he delivered a direct blow.

"We're looking for a certain Julius Lessinger."

Besesti paled and was speechless for some moments, yet his eyes expressed a cruel anguish. He grabbed the table, which teetered.

De Vincenzi went over to him, put a hand on his shoulder and physically forced him to sit down. "Try to pull yourself together, and tell me everything you know. Only then will I be able to protect you effectively."

There was a long pause. The interrogation that followed was one of the most difficult De Vincenzi would have to conduct in the whole of his long career. It was clear that Besesti was afraid of some unknown danger—or known only to himself—which hung over him. All the same, he was disinclined to reveal the secrets of his murky past, one that might constitute just as serious a danger if laid bare. He was subject to moods of pitiful self-abandonment alternating with stubborn, irritable rebellion. De Vincenzi felt things heating up around him. Events were moving forward, and he'd have to hurry. This man was resisting: he was keeping him shut up in a room while a scream might come from outside at any moment, the scream of another victim, a shot from a revolver, the mad wailing of those women… He could have slapped him, and was kept from doing so only by the thought that not even violence would wrench a frank and complete confession from this man.

"Where did you meet Major Alton?"

"In Australia."

"How long ago?"

"Four years, five… I don't know any more. It was when the war broke out."

Those answers came easily, but then he dug his heels in. "Australia, given that it was under the English Crown, was at war. Argentina, no. There was nothing to keep me in Buenos Aires. My company had come through a difficult year, and we weren't doing business any more. We dealt in furs. I had been robbed by my cashier and I left. I had a few projects in mind. I disembarked at Sydney, and it was there that I met Alton and we became business partners." He lost his train of thought again. "We equipped some steamships and were doing some coastal trading around the islands."

De Vincenzi looked him in the face. Did coastal trading mean furnishing German submarines?

"Was Major Alton in the British army?"

"No! What do you mean? What does the British army have to do with anything? Alton was a free man. Oh, yes, you mean his rank. But it was years and years since he'd been in the army. In 1901, after the Boer War, he resigned his commission. In any event, nothing that happened during that time concerns me. I didn't even know him then! I have nothing to do with this. Do you understand? Nothing to do with it!" He was worked up, practically shouting.

De Vincenzi smiled. "I understand. Rest assured. You're not involved. You had no connections with Julius Lessinger."

Besesti threw him a look that might have been either pleading or angry. The look of a cornered beast, pushed to the limit, which doesn't ask for mercy because it knows it's pointless and which lacks the energy for the final pounce.

"Did you and Major Alton act alone in this coastal trading between the islands? Was it a good business?"

"I rebuilt my wealth on the back of it."

"I can believe it. Did you also meet the major's wife during that time?"

Besesti looked at De Vincenzi with surprise. "No. Alton went to Europe. But I knew at the time, in fact, that he'd taken a wife. He was married here in Italy."

A flash of intuition coursed through the inspector.

"The couple stayed in this hotel, am I right?"

"What are you saying? But of course! You're making me think… I swear I don't remember… Yes, definitely. The major must have been here that year because I wrote to him at this address from Sydney. When I got to Milan a few months ago, I came to this hotel precisely because I remembered its name."

"What did Alton do after that?"

"He went back to Australia."

"With his wife?"

"No. He came to Europe to join her for a month or two every year—until 1917. We dissolved our business then, sold the steamships. I stayed a bit longer in Australia, went back to Argentina for a while. Until a few months ago, when I decided to establish myself in Milan."

"In order to set up the Bank of Pure Metals?"

"I didn't know what else to do. I certainly couldn't have stayed there doing nothing. The bank is a healthy business: ten million in capital, all in deposits."

"It's all yours?"

"Yes."

"By Jove! The earnings from your coastal trading must have been really remarkable!"

"You're free to disbelieve it. But no one can dispute the money I have."

"Did Flemington also let you know about the death of Major Alton and the opening of the will, which is to take place here in this hotel, today in fact?"

"Yes, but the information was of no interest to me. I never had and I don't have any reason to believe that Alton's will concerns me."

"Then how do you explain the lawyer's having asked you to come as well?"

"I don't have an explanation."

"What about the death of Douglas Layng?"

"Ah!"

"And the death of Giorgio Novarreno?"

"Has he been killed as well?"

"He was stabbed."

Besesti didn't speak for several minutes. The silence in the room was interrupted only by the sound of water dripping from a tap in the sink, left on or perhaps broken. De Vincenzi noticed it only that moment, and from then on the relentless, penetrating, monotonous noise obsessed him. It was as if the drops were falling soft and muffled on his head.

"No! I cannot see why anyone would kill Novarreno. I knew him. I met him here. But I would never have imagined that that Levantine had any connection with Alton or his heirs."

"Maybe it was he who created one—a tie."

"What do you mean?"

"Do you know Signora Mary Alton?"

"No."

"But Douglas Layng, yes—right?"

"I met him here. It would have been about a month ago."

"What sort of friendship did he have with Major Alton, or how closely related were they? And with Signora Alton?"

"I don't know!" Besesti struggled to get up. Once on his feet, he seemed to recover his pompous demeanour. He looked at the inspector with his blue eyes, still murky and cloudy. "Inspector, this questioning has gone on long enough. I have no right nor any duty to tell you anyone else's secrets. I have nothing to do with the crimes committed in this hotel."

"And with those that are about to be?"

He looked away, and then quickly at the door.

"I don't know what you mean."

De Vincenzi said coldly, "Fine. You know very well what I'm alluding to. It's my duty to protect your life along with everyone else's. Yet although I'm doing everything I can, you're doing nothing to help me! You'll only have yourself to blame."

He turned his back on Besesti and made for the door. He had his hand on the knob when Besesti called out, "Inspector!"

"Well?"

"When Flemington arrives, do let me know. I need to speak with him immediately."

"The meeting with the heirs is fixed for today. Flemington has already arrived in Milan."

"Without saying anything to me! Where is he? Tell me where he is and let me go to him."

"You'll see him shortly." And De Vincenzi left the room, closing the door behind him. He found Sani and the two officers in the corridor.

"The doctor has arrived," Sani told him.

"Put a guard on this door."

De Vincenzi went up to Room 6. Standing in the doorway, he saw the doctor from the emergency medical service there with the body. "The same wound as the other one, Doctor?"

The doctor let out one of those inarticulate sounds which spared him the bother of answering. He got up slowly. He was so tall, he looked like a compass opening out. In his hands he held the switchblade, which he'd extracted from the dead man's chest.

"The same weapon, I believe," he said, turning to De Vincenzi. "It's not easy to find a knife with such a long, thin blade. It reached the heart this time, too." Then his skull-like face tensed and his eyes flashed. "But weren't you and all your men in here when they killed this one? Are you going to let this massacre go on all night?"

De Vincenzi shrugged.

"I'm leaving, and I hope you won't be calling me again to remove more knives from dead men's chests."

De Vincenzi had already left the room and gone down the first flight of stairs. He was hurrying up the steep stairway to the attic rooms while the doctor continued hurling sarcastic barbs at him. Despite the rude and discourteous manner in which they were offered, De Vincenzi felt the doctor's words had something in them. No one would have believed that another man could be killed in this hotel, occupied as it was by police and guards in every corner.

Cruni was sitting on the top step. When he saw the inspector he rose, holding on to the railing.

"Any news?"

"No, sir. They're sleeping in there." He pointed to the maids' room. "I sent the porter away since the room is still occupied by… the body. In the other two rooms there are now two men. But they were talking for a long time, shut up in the first room. It was the fatter one, the one who looks like an elephant, who called the other man as soon as he went into his room. He seemed crazy and panted like a seal. I've no idea what was going on, since they started speaking in English."

He'd seen the porcelain doll: De Vincenzi didn't doubt for an instant that Engel's agitation hinged on that fact. But didn't the doll belong to him? What was the story behind these porcelain dolls that *had* to be brought to Milan, to that hotel, by the will of Harry Alton, who'd advised his wife not to forget her own? *I have reserved a surprise for you that's not the least bit banal…* But then something new had turned up—possibly expected, despite being feared—and the surprises turned macabre. He was about to knock on Engel's door when an idea occurred to him and he stopped.

"Go and get the owner, bring him up here. Hurry!"

Virgilio arrived with Cruni at his heels, urging him to hasten upstairs. The poor man was dizzy with sleep and fear, completely disorientated by the wrath of God which had unexpectedly struck him and his hotel.

"How long have you managed this hotel?" De Vincenzi had to repeat the question in order to be understood.

"Two years." He gave his explanations in broken sentences, now verbose, now struggling to find words. He'd been in charge of a large beer hall in the city centre. He'd found two or three clients there who'd lent him the necessary funds—partly to help him and also believing they were making a good investment—and he'd taken over the business in 1917, agreeing to a ten-year lease with the outgoing hotelier, who still owned the building.

"So in 1914, The Hotel of the Three Roses was managed by…"

"By Bernasconi, a Swiss man who'd founded it thirty years before and had become rich, chiefly because of the restaurant."

"Where is this Bernasconi now?"

"Here, in Milan. He lives in via Solferino. He comes to see me every day. I would prefer him not to come, because—you know—everyone does things their own way, and all he does is criticize and give advice."

"Take him back downstairs and get him to give you the precise address of the old hotelier. Go and get him at seven and bring him here."

He'd hoped that Virgilio would be able to tell him about Major Alton and his wedding at The Three Roses in 1914. There was nothing to do, however, but wait for day to arrive so he could interrogate Bernasconi.

He knocked at Engel's door. Silence at first, then a chair moving, a drawer closing. The man was moving about the room. He knocked again and said, "Open up. I need to speak to you."

The door opened. Vilfredo Engel—huge, sturdy elephant that he was—had put on his white silk pyjamas, so tight he was practically bursting out of them. They pinched at his armpits and across the chest, and hugged his back and legs. The bottoms ended a full six inches above his ankles, leaving his enormous, hairy calves bare. His tiny eyes blazed with bewilderment under bushy grey eyebrows.

"What do you want? Why did you wake me up?"

But he hadn't in fact been sleeping. The bedsheets were turned down in welcome, but it was clear he had not yet lain on them. De Vincenzi stepped into the room while Engel trailed after him awkwardly, waving his hands around to emphasize his objection. But no matter how hard he searched, the inspector could not see a doll. He must have hidden it in a drawer or his suitcase.

"Signor Engel, go back to bed if you wish, or else sit down. I need to speak to you without interruptions."

"But who are you?"

"A policeman. Did you not know that a body was found hanging from an iron bar on the landing just outside your door last night?"

"Have you come to arrest me? In which case I'll say nothing unless my lawyer is present."

"Why should I arrest you? Were you the one who killed Douglas Layng?"

130

"No! I deny it. I didn't even know the poor young man. It's awful. Just because he was hung up outside my room, there's no reason in the world to believe that I have the least thing to do with such an atrocious crime."

"Calm down. No one is accusing you of having killed Layng. But to say that you did not know him is a lie. Let's not waste time. It will be better for you and for me."

"I have nothing to do with it! I protest! I have the right to the assistance of a lawyer."

But he sat down, and the chair squawked under his weight. With his hands on his knees, his shoulders rounded and his pointy head bent backward so he could keep an eye on De Vincenzi, he seemed like a gigantic monkey whose trainer had goaded him into putting on that silly white costume for amusement's sake.

"Was William Engel your brother?"

"Yes."

"When did he die?"

"In 1902."

"In South Africa?"

"No, in London. In my arms."

"He was an officer in Major Alton's battalion?"

"Yes."

De Vincenzi paused for some time.

"Would you repeat to me what your brother confided to you before dying?"

Engel blinked.

"Would you tell me about Julius Lessinger?"

He went on questioning, affecting indifference to the questions, yet watching for their effect on the man's face. However, it wasn't possible for Engel's face, stiff and leathery as it was, to twitch or betray his feelings. De Vincenzi could only try reading

131

his eyes, and he did this accurately, subtly, beadily: two shining points between half-closed eyelids.

"It's an old story you're asking about. I'd hoped it was buried for ever."

"What if I told you that Julius Lessinger had killed Douglas Layng?"

"*Impossible!*"

"Why? Who else could have wanted that young man to die?"

"Who else?" He sniggered and then began to pant again in that way of his, with his lips and cheeks puffed out.

"Who was Douglas Layng?"

"The son of—" He stopped and reached out for the drawer. "There's a bottle of cognac in there. May I offer you a glass?"

"Douglas Layng was the son of? Go on. Do you want me to complete your sentence? He was the son of Major Alton."

He began to snigger once again. "If you already know…"

"What about his mother?"

"What gentleman would reveal such a secret? Because you find me in this shabby room on the top floor of a third-rate hotel, you think you have the right to insult me?"

What patience! But he wasn't trying to be devious in order to avoid being questioned. It was worse than that: he was devious by nature.

"Look, Engel. Try to understand the seriousness of the moment, of all that has happened and might happen. How do you explain the body's being placed on this landing right outside your room?"

"It's the most out-of-the-way corner in the hotel for carrying out a crime, this is. The youth would have been dragged up here on some pretext. Don't you see that this is a real dump? They don't even light the rooms properly, by God!"

"He wasn't hanged up here. Douglas Layng was stabbed hours before, then dressed and brought up to this landing and hung from the rope."

Engel let out a sort of grunt. He might have been upset—but how could one tell?

"They would have known you would not have been able to avoid seeing him when you came up to your room that night."

"Me?"

He made as if to get up, but fell back into the chair; it groaned. He drew back and looked around the room.

"All set up for me…"

"And look what they dropped at the bottom of those stairs."

De Vincenzi took the small piece of folded paper from his pocket, the one Sani had picked up on the first landing of the stairway. He read: *"The first: the youngest, the innocent. This isn't a warning. It's the beginning of a series."*

"Give it here!" Engel practically tore it from De Vincenzi's hand and looked at it closely. He was frightened. He held the paper for several moments, still looking at it and panting continuously, gasping for breath. Suddenly he burst into laughter—coarse, raucous and punctuated by phlegmy coughs. There were tears in his eyes.

"What's the matter? Why are you laughing like this?"

"Extraordinary, and all of you fell for it! Julius Lessinger, eh? Crocodiles! Revenge! A box full of diamonds! Now you'll bring out all the details of that story that obsessed Harry Alton in the last years of his life. Ah! The man hanged up here in order to terrify me!"

"But that young man *was* killed. And not only him."

"Of course he was killed. But first, it's not at all certain that Lessinger is in Italy. And this paper is enough to show that

133

Lessinger doesn't have anything to do with the murder." He laughed and laughed, murmuring "Imbeciles!" between guffaws.

De Vincenzi was overcome by a strange sense of the surreal, the fantastic. Madness.

"Lessinger has never been to Italy! He has always lived in Africa and Australia. *He can't write in Italian, Lessinger!* And he couldn't have learnt it in a few days, since he could hardly write in English!" He stopped. He seemed to have pulled himself together. He offered the sheet of paper to the inspector and got up. "The whole thing is a farce! Like putting that doll on my bed… Damned Da Como! He performs the tricks and the others take advantage of them."

Whenever De Vincenzi had occasion to recount this scene later, he'd say: "If I didn't go crazy in that room, I'll never go crazy again in my entire life. Since, you see, *if there weren't already two people dead, one might still have been laughing!* But there *were* two bodies, and only a few minutes later there would be a third, *and I already knew who it would be.*"

14

Engel was sitting on the bed, still in his white pyjamas, his legs sticking out of them and red slippers dangling from his bare feet. De Vincenzi stood in the middle of the room staring at Carlo Da Como, who'd stayed near the door. Dressed once more in collar and tie, Da Como had had to wait to be questioned. He knew all too well that this awful story was just beginning. He managed to appear calm, perhaps even indifferent, but he was profoundly worried. It was he who'd put the porcelain doll on Engel's bed—he'd already confessed during a stormy conversation with his friend and he confirmed it now to the inspector. But how could he have known that, as soon as he'd gone down to the dining room, someone would bring a body up to the third floor and hang it on the landing? A tragic trick of fate...

"Have you known Engel a long time?"

"Years and years. We met in London. We lived in the same boarding house."

"Why don't you say that the house was yours, Carlo?"

Engel's voice was deep and hoarse. He was no longer chortling, but at that moment he doubled up with laughter, abandoning himself to mirth as if to shake off the terror that had overcome him at De Vincenzi's revelation. It was followed by a state of meditative, searching prostration. It was clear that he was making a desperate effort to understand *what* was happening and *why* it was happening.

Da Como shrugged. "Inspector, it's better if I explain it quickly. At one time I was rich. A long time ago. My father left a considerable estate and I was the only son, with three sisters. I frittered it all away. I was crazy about horse-racing in London. The bookmakers pocketed the better part of my money. Then there were the women. So, if you look for information about me, downstairs they'll talk about my drug-dealing, about a Soho den, about my hotel where there was gambling…" He shrugged again. "All exaggerations. But I might as well tell you myself. I lived as I pleased, it's true. And I learnt to my cost that any kind of life is difficult and one has to fight, armed and always ready to bear the cost personally. At the beginning, as a young man, I was innocent of this, with my own illusions, and people took advantage of me. When I no longer had anything, I did in turn what I'd seen others do: I killed off all my weaknesses and abandoned my scruples. There you have it." He paused, waiting for the inspector to speak. But De Vincenzi kept quiet. Cruni could be heard pacing on the landing outside the room.

"None of this, though, has anything to do with that man's murder, or anything else. Engel came to live in my boarding house. We're friends. A few months ago when I suggested that I might return to Italy, it was he who immediately said he'd come with me, and he who brought me to this hotel, which I didn't even know existed. It's true that these days I'm living here hand to mouth. When I gamble and win, I pay my account here. But now I'm waiting to be hired by the Bank of Pure Metals. Engel introduced me to Signor Besesti."

"It's true," the fat man uttered in his rough, deep voice.

De Vincenzi suddenly turned to him. "So during the war you were involved with Alton and Besesti in their… coastal trading business, right?"

"What do you mean? I have never been in business with Major Alton. I wouldn't even have met him if he hadn't come to see me after my brother died."

"Why did he come to see you?"

"Because he wanted me to give him the porcelain doll." It came out spontaneously, and he immediately regretted it. He seemed angry. "Damn those dolls and the rest of it. My brother died of a broken heart on their account. He was poisoned by the memory."

"Wasn't he, instead, afraid of Lessinger's revenge?"

De Vincenzi was groping around in the dark, trying to latch on to some piece of the story he'd overlooked, something the others were revealing only in fragments, stray details that didn't make sense. The crocodiles on the River Vaal, the dolls, Julius Lessinger, the memory of whom caused everyone to tremble... And the very fact of the gathering at The Hotel of the Three Roses, where a dead man's will had convened everyone directly or indirectly connected to whatever he'd done—probably with the complicity of his two officers during the terrible years of his stay in the Transvaal... The box of diamonds... The soldier, Lessinger...

Engel took De Vincenzi's blow without reacting. "Old story."

"Yet it's necessary to understand it all now, that story." He turned to face Da Como. "So how did you know about the doll's existence? Why did you want to *play a joke* on your friend by putting it on his bed?"

"I told you: we lived together. Do you think I could forget the fact that, amongst his things, Engel had a porcelain doll in a little pink slip? To begin with, I thought it was a memento of a child of his—faraway or dead. But he told me he hadn't had children. I asked him about the doll, then, and he gave me some vague answer. But one night in London, we'd drunk a lot of whisky—"

"I was the only one drinking!" came the deep, hoarse voice of the man in white pyjamas.

"Are you saying I took advantage of your drunkenness in order to squeeze the secret out of you?" Da Como's eyes were blazing, and he clenched his fists so hard that his knuckles went white. Engel merely shrugged in response. "Answer me! What do you want the inspector to think?" Anger swelled the tendons in Da Como's neck, and his large face went scarlet. His reaction seemed excessive, or at least way out of proportion to Engel's statement, which had appeared completely innocent and lacking malice. "Don't believe him! We were both drunk and he started talking. He told me a terrible story. His brother, along with Major Alton and Captain Nolan, committed a horrendous crime."

"William was only twenty, a kid. He was just out of artillery training and they sent him into combat. A boy… The other two were the ones who committed the crime, and against him, poor thing—he died of it two years later."

It didn't seem possible that this huge man with bronzed skin was softening. But his voice sounded harsher and deeper than ever and it was with difficulty that he forced the words from a tight throat.

De Vincenzi listened, attentive to the smallest movement of the two men. At last someone had decided to speak. But the two kept quiet, as if they'd realized only now that a third man was there, watching and listening. Engel shot Da Como a look of hatred from those great gimlet eyes underneath his bushy grey eyebrows.

"And the doll?" De Vincenzi asked coldly. Da Como kept quiet. "The doll?" he repeated.

He didn't want to give them any time for reflection. He was hoping one would talk if he pitted them against each another. There had to be something there. Da Como's anger towards the huge man in white had not yet cooled. Perhaps that was how he dominated Engel, constantly threatening him with revealing the secret wrung from him during a night of drinking, and he feared losing his hold over him. Maybe it was blackmail, and had been going on for years. Drug-dealing... the Soho den... the hotel where they'd gambled... The man had raised his hands so the inspector wouldn't ask him anything about London. However, De Vincenzi didn't have time to contact Scotland Yard. Everything would need to be resolved within the next few hours. If he did not arrest the killer before the hotel reopened for business, he couldn't hope to catch him. On the other hand, it wasn't possible for him to hold all these people in broad daylight. In a few hours the investigating magistrate would initiate the routine enquiries, and the wheels of bureaucracy would begin to grind.

"The doll?"

"When all's said and done, it's nothing to do with me!" Now it was Da Como who didn't want the truth to come out.

"Engel, I'm aware of two porcelain dolls like yours now, the one I saw on your bed there, and another one which Mary Alton has in her room." The man did not move. He knew very well that the widow had arrived and he couldn't be unaware that she too had a porcelain doll dressed in pink. "If you won't tell me the whole truth, then the *signora* will. And don't forget that there are other people who'll speak: Flemington and his wife."

Engel stirred. "Flemington's arrived?"

"Some time ago."

He panted rapidly before rising from the edge of the bed. In his straining pyjamas, he looked absurdly ridiculous.

"Let me get some cognac. I'll tell you the story."

The floor shook under his heavy steps as he made for the dresser and took a bottle from the top drawer. The glass was waiting on top of it, next to his shaving brush and the rest of his shaving kit. He filled it and drank noisily, greedily. He must have been drinking when De Vincenzi had first knocked at his door, and what he'd heard had been the noise of a drawer hurriedly closed in an attempt to hide the bottle.

Propped up by the dresser, he began speaking, turning to De Vincenzi and completely ignoring the presence of Da Como, who was also standing there in front of him, leaning against the door frame.

"In any case, it's a short story. My brother told it to me an hour before he died. But I need to explain something to you, because not everyone knows what sort of life he led down there in South Africa. When Harry Alton went there in 1880, Alton was young and free. He enlisted only later, when war broke out against the Boers. He'd gone to Africa to seek his fortune and arrived in Kimberley just when Cecil Rhodes was setting up the De Beers Company, delivering the final blow to thousands of individual diamond-miners and creating a state monopoly on the gems. One could no longer prosper. Alton understood this so well that he immediately left Kimberley and made for Johannesburg. Mining was still allowed there. Claims were assigned by competition and diggers could try their luck." He spoke in his rough, low voice, struggling, as if teaching a lesson, to choose the right words and feeling gratified by their effect.

"Anyone who believes the prospectors on the banks of the Vaal were a gang of cowboys—like the gold-miners in

California, Australia and Alaska—is mistaken. The diggers on the Vaal were the best of the white immigrants from the Cape Colony. They were students, retired officers, civil servants, distinguished *clubmen*. Real gentlemen, in fact. When he arrived there, Alton was lucky enough to land a claim and he immediately established a firm with his two companions." He stopped and looked at De Vincenzi maliciously. "You'd like to know their names, right, Inspector? You think the names will help you understand everything. So here they are: Dick Nolan and Donald Lessinger."

"So what about Julius Lessinger?"

"He's the son, of course. The son who swore to get rid of everyone, and who was Harry Alton's real nightmare from the day he learnt of his existence. That, however, did not stop him dying in peace from illness and old age in Sydney, finally playing the rest of us for fools and gathering us here in this hotel for the reading of the will in the presence of the three dolls. Because there are three of them, not just two. That girl downstairs will have the third: Dick Nolan's niece, Carin Nolan."

"Listen to me, Engel!" De Vincenzi interrupted heatedly. "You have no idea what danger hangs over some of the other people staying here, but it's real, and it's very serious. What you've told me confirms it, even though it's only the beginning of the story. This is why I'm urging you to hurry! It may be that in what you're about to tell me I'll find some aspect—a clue—that will help me identify and reveal the killer before another crime is committed. Will you keep your words to an absolute minimum?"

Engel fixed on the inspector's mouth as he spoke, like a deaf person trying to understand.

"You still think that Julius Lessinger will be found here carrying out the slaughter!" He shook his head and shoulders vigorously and turned to pour himself another glass of cognac. He knocked it back in his loud, gurgling way, wiping his mouth afterwards with the back of his hand.

"Hmph! It's almost finished. The claim that yielded most was Lessinger's. But he didn't want to say anything yet. The company stipulated an equal division of profits. The fact is, however, that Lessinger knew how to get the better of his partners, who were somewhat younger and less experienced than he was, and he managed to corral into his claim all the best stones and most of the money they brought. Alton and Nolan realized somewhat on the late side that their partner had taken the lion's share. They'd worked for around twenty years and both were as poor as they'd been when they'd come to Kimberley. Lessinger swore that he, too, was poor, but it was with a real sense of relief that he saw his partners enlist under the English flag, and if he couldn't stop his son Julius leaving for war as well, he himself held back from following them. He stayed with his three daughters, then just babies, on the banks of the River Vaal.

"The war was long and bloody. Alton became a major and was put in charge of a light battalion, with complete freedom of action and movement. He had Nolan with him as captain, and my brother, who joined them from England, as lieutenant."

"The crime, Engel—get to the crime!"

He drank some more. All that alcohol was making his eyes glow, and when he began to speak again his tongue was thick and slurred.

"The crime! Oh, the crime was simple, like sucking an egg. Alton must have planned it for a long time, in every detail. He led his battalion along the Vaal and stopped it west of Johannesburg, on a clearing encircled by a wood. Lessinger's house was in the thick of the trees. Alton clearly understood old Lessinger's power and cunning, because he didn't consider Nolan's help or complicity sufficient. He wanted William's as well. He got William drunk on promise, dazzled him with the splendour of all those African gemstones. He was only twenty years old, that boy, and they threw him into a ferocious war with no quarter. How could he have retained a sense of what was honest and good, when he was so intoxicated with slaughter? He went too!

"All three reached Lessinger's house at night. They shot the old man and his three daughters with a revolver. They hung up his body from the ceiling of his hut to make it appear a Boer crime, and threw the babies' bodies to the crocodiles in the river. They found the box with the diamonds… The old man really did have them, and a lot of them, enough to constitute a fortune. Alton buried the box in the wood in the presence of Nolan and my brother. It was impossible to take it with them in the campaign they were leading against the Boers. Whoever survived was to come and get the diamonds. Nolan made the observation that he had a daughter in England, and that his heirs would be entitled… and the three of them swore that if one of them died, and even if only one of them remained alive, the heirs would have their due at his death."

Engel delivered the last part of his tale with difficulty. He tried to drink some more, but couldn't. His eyes were closing. He breathed effortfully, almost wheezing, and he slowly slid down the dresser to the floor, his conical head drooping, his eyes closed, his lower lip hanging loose. De Vincenzi looked at Da Como. The man was pale. He tried to smile but only managed a sinister sneer.

"Did you know this story as well?"

"Yes. He was in this same state when he recounted it to me."

"Help me get him onto the bed."

It was a difficult undertaking. Engel weighed over two hundred pounds. By the time they'd laid him out as best they could on the iron bed, they were both exhausted. They had to stay still for a moment to catch their breath. Da Como went to get a tumbler from the sink and filled it with cognac. De Vincenzi watched him drink without stopping him. Even he could have done with a drink. Recounted like that in the deep, raucous voice of a man who looked like an orangutan dressed up as a clown, and in a room with whitewashed walls, by the pink light of a dusty lamp, the story had profoundly depressed him.

"What about the dolls? Do you know how they come into it?"

"Yes. It's the most dreadful part of the story. The three dolls belonged to the little girls, Lessinger's daughters. They were found on the floor of the room where the slaughter had taken place. Alton gathered them up and gave one to Nolan, the other to William Engel, to serve as proof of identity in case there should be any heirs to inherit the diamonds."

"Did the diamonds remain in Alton's hands?"

"It seems so. Nolan died in battle in 1900 and William Engel left Africa before the war ended. He went to London to be with his brother, and he too died shortly afterwards. I met him. He really was a young boy, and taking part in that awful massacre must have unhinged him."

That explained everything—apart from the murder of Douglas Layng and Giorgio Novarreno. Alton had taken the diamonds and become rich. He'd settled in Australia, and in 1914 he'd supplied German submarines with petrol and coal, and they'd torpedoed the ships of the English and their allies. And he'd been an Englishman... He'd made Besesti his partner that time. But how had that Argentine—himself penniless and just out of bankruptcy in Buenos Aires—got involved with Alton, already rich and not in need of help? By what means had he insinuated himself into that misbegotten company doing despicable work for dishonourable profit?

"And Julius Lessinger?"

"Ah, the son, eh? Engel must know more than he wanted to say. He's never spoken about him to me. Only once, a few years ago, in London… after Major Alton made a visit to *my* hotel, he sneered, '*The old man is terrified because he's got it into his head that Lessinger knows every detail about the death of his father and sisters and has sworn revenge. He wanted me to give him my doll, because he was afraid that the young man might come to see me and spot it. He's a sly fox, but I'm no fool. I've never used the doll against him. But to ask me to give it back!*'"

"Who was Douglas Layng's father?"

"Alton. Engel assured me of that."

"His mother?"

"He would never tell me that."

"And Carin Nolan?"

"I told you—she's the daughter of Dick Nolan's son. Her father is dead and her mother lives in London. The girl arrived here at nearly the same time as Layng, but they pretended not to know each other—or maybe they really didn't."

De Vincenzi looked at his watch: it was a few minutes before six. Outside, the water kept falling drearily, thick as hail, down the zinc guttering. Cruni had stopped pacing on the landing. And the others? He felt frazzled. It was the hardest hour after a night without sleep spent in continual nervous tension, the hour when the body refuses to stand up straight, the brain seems liquefied, and the cerebellum at the back of the neck burns as if punctured by flaming needles. After that, one picks up. But at that hour, one's forces are drained and one feels like throwing oneself on the floor just to rest. He had to act, however. The worst was yet to come.

"That's fine. Go back to your room. I'll call for you if I need you."

Da Como glanced at the sleeping Engel, who was still snorting loudly under the influence of alcohol—a monstrous carnival puppet. He turned to go, but stopped when he got to the door.

"Do you believe that young Layng's body was hung on this landing in order to frighten Engel?"

"I don't believe anything."

The other man paused. "Has anyone told you there's a built-in wardrobe on this corridor, a sort of hiding place?"

"No! Where is it?"

"It's difficult to make the door out in this light if you don't know it's there."

In fact the door was there, on the part of the corridor that led to Engel's and Da Como's rooms. It shut simply, with a spring latch. De Vincenzi opened it and had to use the torch Sani had given him to look inside. A glory hole where the maids and the porter kept rags and brooms. It would have been impossible to keep a body hidden there all afternoon, to say nothing of the difficulty of carrying it up the main staircase, then the smaller one in plain daylight, while downstairs the hotel guests, the maids and Signora Maria and Virgilio came and went. De Vincenzi shone the torch along the walls and on the bottom, and rummaged in the corners: spiders, dust. A mouse darted between his feet and fled down the corridor.

All at once, he saw something shining through the dust. He knelt down and picked up a gold circle with three concentric circles of red and blue enamel. Half of a cufflink.

"Did you find something?"

The inspector closed the door, turned the key in the lock and put it in his pocket.

"Go to your room."

It was a few minutes before he went downstairs. On the way he passed Cruni, sleeping on the last step, his head and shoulders against the wall.

15

Halfway down the other part of the first-floor corridor, De Vincenzi heard the tap-tap of a typewriter. A strange sound, to tell the truth—jerky and uneven. *A really old one, and he's the only one who can actually manage to write with it…* What in the world could Bardi, the hunchback, be typing at that hour?

The part of Engel's story that featured Da Como had revealed a lot to him. The various people involved in the tragedy were beginning to assume clean outlines, to come to life in their contexts, illuminated by their pasts. But he still couldn't see it all clearly. How had the atrocious murder of Douglas Layng been carried out? And above all, how had it been possible to keep the body hidden for an entire afternoon? What diabolical skill had allowed someone to carry him from the room where he'd been kept up to the top floor, seizing on the moment when everyone else in the hotel was in the dining room or outside the building? Did that half-cufflink found in the wardrobe mean the body had been hidden there? Absurd. Then had the killer hidden in it? Did the cufflink belong to the killer? Above all, he struggled to understand why someone had wanted to hang the body from the landing and leave the pencil-written note, all in capitals, lying at the foot of the stairs. *For whom* had the drama been staged, and *at whom* was that terrifyingly brief message directed?

He went past Stella Essington's room, Douglas Layng's, the one belonging to Novarreno, who was still lying where the killer had found him, past Pompeo Besesti's room and Nicola Al Righetti's. He looked in the corner at the door to Room 12, Mary Alton Vendramini's room. Were they all there, locked inside, each in his or her own cage, the players in this drama? He stopped in front of the door to Room 9, Carin Nolan's room. Nineteen years old. Another porcelain doll. That woman was probably one of the designated victims, and along with her, Mary Alton. And then in the blue room downstairs—the man with the whisky in front of him, the woman stretched out on the sofa enjoying a troubled sleep full of nightmares and anxiety: the Flemington couple. All of them were threatened. He knew it, and from one moment to the next he was expecting someone to come and tell him about some new drama.

But how? It was the tap-tap of the typewriter that drew him from his contemplation and led him to Room 9. Why did he think that the number 9 was a cabbalistic number, a perfect number? He heard the strident but alternately warm and harmonious voice of Giorgio Novarreno telling him the inscrutable names of his divinatory practices: aeromancy, daphnomancy, lampadomancy. The dead man would practise none of them any more.

The tapping of the typewriter continued. Another anonymous letter? What did Stefano Bardi know?

He made up his mind. He quickly walked the last part of the corridor and went to knock on the door of the watch-seller. The machine stopped immediately. He heard a chair move. The sound of steps. The door opened: an enormous spider with endless, skinny legs. He, too, was completely dressed. Waiting. He was terribly white in the face, terribly, and a tuft of mousy

149

hair was falling over his forehead. His glaucous eyes were filled with terror and looked watery, with hundreds of tiny specks. He asked nothing, simply stepped back. It seemed to De Vincenzi that Bardi was relieved to recognize him. Perhaps he had been expecting someone he was afraid of…

"It's me again, Signor Bardi."

The room was small and full of boxes and small cases, all piled up against the walls, between the four legs of the table, maybe even under the bed… On the table, the typewriter, a sheaf of documents gathered together in colourful folders. De Vincenzi sat down near the table in the only chair. Pretending to look around the room, he immediately began trying to read the paper in the typewriter.

"I was writing a business letter."

Slowly De Vincenzi took the anonymous letter out of his pocket, unfolded it and compared the characters to those on the sheet in the typewriter. *Veuillez bien m'envoyer une Longines en or serie A.B.F. 22270… There's a place in Milan where people gamble furiously all night…* Identical! The same "i" missing its dot, the same one-sided "n", the same wonky character alignment.

The hunchback watched him without moving. The only thing he did was to go and lean on the headboard of the bed, threading his hands through the iron decorations as if to support himself.

"Signor Bardi, why did you write this letter and send it to police headquarters?"

De Vincenzi spoke in a gentle voice, placing the letter on the table nonchalantly, as if to suggest that he attached no importance to it.

"Are you actually certain that I wrote it?" Bardi replied for the sake of saying something, and to gain time.

"Oh don't worry about it! Your intentions were good and events have borne them out. You wanted to warn someone, to prevent everything that's happened and is about to happen."

"I don't know anything. I don't."

"This is another matter, don't you think? If you wanted to alert the authorities and let them know about the danger looming over the people in this hotel, why are you refusing to speak now? If you speak now, you can save a human life—maybe more than one."

"What do you mean?"

"That the killer has not yet finished his work. The murder of Douglas Layng was but the first, and I'm of the opinion that Giorgio Novarreno's was entirely random. Look, I'm being completely open with you."

Bardi sat up straight. "What are you saying? Have they killed Novarreno too?"

"Didn't you know?" the inspector asked frankly. "Oh! Then perhaps—but what's wrong? Are you feeling ill?"

He had to run to support Bardi. He took his arm and laid him out on the bed. How strangely light he was! A boy would have weighed more. He was panting and his cheeks were aflame, two scarlet dots on that wan, spiteful and emaciated face. He got him to drink, and the water ran down his chin onto his neck. He blinked. Little by little he recovered himself and sat upright, his feet on the floor. De Vincenzi tried to stop him, convinced that he was about to run off.

"Novarreno," he uttered. "Him too! Oh! And I thought—" He stopped mid-sentence and bit his lip.

De Vincenzi looked severe. "Bardi, it's time to break your silence! This game can't go on, and I'll stop it at any cost. Do you understand? At any cost. What do you know? What have

151

you seen? Who is terrorizing you to such an extent that you refuse to speak?" He looked at Bardi in desperation.

"I don't know anything. I don't know any of these people. Why did I write that letter? It was wrong of me. I shouldn't have got mixed up in it. But I felt sorry for that creature. I saw that she was about to make a mistake. Such a good person, so beautiful! It tore at my heartstrings. I even tried to speak to her, but I didn't manage it. What would she have thought of me if I had told her she shouldn't trust that man's attentions? In the end, I didn't even know who he was. Cocaine… yes, I saw that. But she refused to take it. She started laughing! He immediately put it back in his pocket, trying to pretend it was all a joke. Was it enough for me to tell her that I'd seen his glances, that I was petrified of them? *It wasn't a joke*, but how could I prove it to her? And then—me. The person she never thought worthy of a second look! So I wrote. I did the wrong thing. But the man who was hung up… Novarreno… all the rest of it. No. No! I don't know anything. And I'd never have imagined that here in this hotel, after all the years I've lived here… What do you want? I'm alone in this world. I'd begun to think of this place as my home and the people living here as my family! No. If anyone had told me I was going to have such a nightmarish time here, I'd never have believed it."

Even in his agitated state, pouring out that pitiful story, he used the sort of melodramatic phrases you'd find in romantic novels read by seamstresses. He was a sentimentalist of a rather morbid sensitivity who got upset or crushed or overexcited with all his fretting. How often had he lain on that small bed with its pillow, his hump shaking with lovelorn sobs over some woman who was avoiding him and who'd got close to him perhaps only to touch his deformity for good luck? De Vincenzi felt boundless pity for this poor human being, all alone in the world. However, what really mattered to him was that this wreck of a man actually knew a lot.

"OK, fine, Signor Bardi. You have nothing to do with any of this. And after all, the nightmare will pass. What's done is done, unfortunately. The dead don't come back. But human justice does exist, and it must act to defend society. So apart from all else, I must do everything I can to prevent there being further victims, and you need to help me. So, the threatened innocent is—"

The other man listened to him, trying to calm down and stop his panting. But he was gripping the white bedcover, and every now and again threw a terrified look at the half-open door. De Vincenzi went over to close it, turned the key in the lock, and returned to Bardi.

"There are policemen in the corridor. You have nothing to fear. Tell me—the woman you mentioned is... Carin Nolan?"

His face was lit up and his eyes gleamed desperately. "Protect her!" he burst out loftily, the words betraying his secret.

"From whom? Who is *threatening* her? Who is courting her and offering her cocaine?"

He fell into a frenzy. He began kicking the air and thrashing about. He slid to the ground and started rolling around, battering the corners of the furniture with his head and feet, his mouth foaming. Ten minutes went by while De Vincenzi struggled with someone possessed, pitying him and wanting more than anything to avoid harming him. He finally managed to get him back on the bed—and if Bardi was shattered, exhausted, De Vincenzi was too. He stood up and smoothed out his suit and tie, which had got mussed up during the struggle. There was a mirror above the sink, and De Vincenzi caught

153

in it the signs of total exhaustion on his face: he had deep, dark circles under his eyes and the lines at the corners of his mouth had deepened. He sighed and then smiled resignedly. This was his job.

He looked at his watch: a quarter to seven. It would be day before long. What else was about to happen? What else *had* happened which he didn't yet know about? He was overwhelmed by panic for several moments; he felt there was no escape. He'd have to get a firm grip, and since he had nerves of steel he managed to control himself. But a dark, elusive and vague foreboding stayed with him. He had to act, whatever the cost.

He walked over to the door and as he reached for the knob, he noticed that Bardi's eyes were open, staring at him. He heard a whisper as he spoke without moving his lips.

"It's my illness. This time it went off by itself. Will you give me my sedative, please?" He held out his hand and pointed to the chest of drawers.

What a hand! De Vincenzi looked at it, fascinated: long and simian, with large white bumps for knuckles. He had to force himself to look away. On the dresser he spotted a bottle with a yellow label, along with a spoon. He gave Bardi the potion. While his back was turned so he could replace the bottle and spoon on the dresser, the other man spoke.

"Go ahead and question me. I'll tell you what I know."

De Vincenzi turned round and saw that Bardi was pale enough to cause concern, his eyes closed. He realized he'd have to take advantage of this moment of debilitating depression. He would have to be quick about it.

"The man's name?"

"The American—Al Righetti."

"Did they arrive at the hotel at the same time, he and Carin Nolan?"

"No—the American was here a month before her."

"And he was courting her?"

"Yes."

"What did she do?"

Bardi's lips tensed in a painful smile.

"She… I think she liked him."

"Did you write the letter just because the American was wooing Carin?"

"No. There's gambling here. It's a corrupt place. Lots of women are taking cocaine. Well, one day I was behind the glass wall that separates the dining room from the lobby. I saw the American open a little silver box and offer some white powder to Carin to sniff. I realized that he wanted to corrupt her, ruin her. That's when I wrote the message."

"When was that?"

"Two or three days ago. I wrote the letter the same night that all this happened."

"What does Al Righetti do?"

"I don't know. I don't think he does anything. He's got money."

"Do you know Engel?"

"I don't believe so."

"Da Como?"

"Yes, I know him. They must have met in London. They talked a few times in front of the others about some shared experiences in London."

"Who is the American especially friendly with?"

"No one. He hardly spoke to anyone at first."

"But to women?"

"He must have had—a certain intimacy with Stella Essington. But from the moment Douglas Layng arrived, she attached herself to him, and Al Righetti moved off right away."

"What do you know about Besesti?"

"What does he have to do with anything? He's rich. He rarely frequented the downstairs room. I never saw him gambling."

"Does Besesti know someone here—in some special way? I mean, is he friendly with anyone?"

"Engel. Sometimes he even goes up to his room, right up to the top." And he trembled at the memory of what he'd seen up there.

"What interests do you think they have in common?"

"Besesti must have given money to the Englishman, but not as a loan... I don't know. Maybe he owed him something. It seemed to me that they had known each other for some time."

"What about Novarreno?"

"The Levantine didn't know Besesti. I mean, he knew him like everyone else did. That charlatan always found some way to speak to people if he wanted to. No one escaped him. But as for intimacy..."

"Bardi"—after a brief pause, De Vincenzi's voice grew serious—"where were you yesterday afternoon?"

"I had to go out right after breakfast to see some clients. But I was back in the hotel at four."

"Where?"

"Here." A smile, and he went on. "They'll have told you that I'm constantly roaming around the hotel, that I stick my nose in other people's business. You want to know about that, don't you? Yesterday I stayed in my room. I didn't feel well."

"Carin Nolan?"

Struggling, he replied, "She went out with Al Righetti. She came back at six."

"Are you sure she went out with the American?"

"I believe so. I heard them talking in the corridor around six. But it could be that she went out on her own and they just met up in the corridor."

"What time did you go down to the dining room yesterday evening?"

"A little after seven."

"Did you notice anything unusual in the corridor?"

"Nothing."

"Why did you go up to the third floor yesterday evening? Tell me the truth!"

"I thought a man had gone through the door on the first landing downstairs, the one with the other staircase leading up to the third floor. I was at the bottom of the main staircase, almost in the lobby. I heard someone coming down, but the steps halted at the first landing and no one appeared. I thought it was the porter going to find the maid. I realize that my curiosity was a bit obsessive! I waited about ten minutes before going up myself. That's when I saw the body."

Had the killer carried the body upstairs at just that moment? Were those ten minutes enough for him to have put the rope over the bar and hung up the body? Or was he going back upstairs after having carried out the procedure *to give it the finishing touch*, to take care of some detail? Had he heard Bardi coming up and hidden in that built-in wardrobe... the cufflink... then, taking advantage of the momentary panic caused by the hunchback's scream, hurried downstairs? Yes, it all stood up. But once downstairs, how could he have entered the dining room without being noticed?

In any case, if he had to accept this scenario—for now, completely bizarre—*then no one who was in the dining room when*

Bardi sounded the alarm could be guilty. He recalled the faces of each person he'd seen locked up in there. Hadn't he said to Inspector Bianchi that there was no one in the first-floor rooms? And no one had gone in later... He began to wrack his brains over the seemingly insoluble problem, and hurriedly continued his questioning. There was one more point he wanted to clear up—an important one.

"How many years have you lived at the Three Roses, Bardi?"

"Ten years. Before that I worked in Lausanne. I came to Milan in 1909 and happened upon this place right away."

"So you were here in 1914?"

"Yes, why?"

"Did you notice the woman in mourning who arrived yesterday?"

"Signora Alton Vendramini?" Bardi had propped himself up on his elbows and was looking at the inspector.

"That's the one. Did you know her?"

"Ah, yes! I was sure I'd seen her some other time. I actually said so to Signora Maria. That's it! 1914, did you say? Yes. I was living in this hotel then, but she didn't go by the name of Alton Vendramini. No, I don't think that was her name."

"Was she alone?"

He almost shouted. "But she got married here, that lady, I'm sure of it! She married Major Alton, an Englishman quite a bit older. Everyone was laughing about it. The wedding caused an uproar in the hotel, not least because it was held in the Protestant church in Piazza Missori, and she—the lady—was Catholic."

"Do you remember any other details?"

"No. They left the day after they were married."

"And before that?"

"The lady was here for a few weeks before the major arrived. They knew each other, and she was waiting for him. They got married immediately."

"You don't remember anything else? The people with whom she socialized before the major arrived, what sort of things she was doing? Anything else?"

"How do you think I can remember? Five years have passed. I've seen so many people in here!" He fell back down on the pillow and closed his eyes.

De Vincenzi watched him for a few moments before opening the door and leaving the room. Had Bardi told him everything he knew? The most pressing problem at the moment was keeping Carin Nolan safe. He'd made up his mind while questioning the hunchback. And he'd concocted a plan. He didn't know anything yet—not a thing. But whether or not it was because of the dawn light, a hypothesis was forming in his mind. The theory was worthless, however, without any evidence. But it was clear that Carin Nolan was in grave danger, and the closer it got to Mr Flemington's reading of the will to the heirs of Harry Alton, the more serious things became. So De Vincenzi decided to get her out of the hotel. He would persuade her to accept his hospitality for a few hours and accompany her to his house, entrusting her to the care of the good Antonietta, his old housekeeper. It was completely illegal as a precaution, and absolutely unprecedented. But for as long as he could he would disregard rules, regulations and legality. He was a good man, and determined to adapt the means to the circumstances.

He knocked at the door of Room 9. No response. He was so agitated and his premonition of evil so strong that he waited no more than a few seconds before turning the handle and opening the door.

The room was dark, but the tomblike silence that reigned over it immediately gave him a sensation of doom. He turned on the light switch and looked at the bed, then ran back to the corridor and called Sani and the officers, shouting their names in a harsh voice.

The body of a woman lay on the bed, and in the middle of a large, red stain on her chest was something shiny. Under a mass of black hair, her face was waxen.

16

De Vincenzi was rigid with tension. The Green Cross stretcher had just that moment taken Carin Nolan away; the assassin's blow had not killed her. This time he hadn't used the switchblade and the blow, dealt by long scissors, had failed to reach her heart. The young woman was unconscious, but she wasn't dead and there was hope that she might be saved. De Vincenzi wished for it with all his being. He felt rather guilty about the most recent attempt. Why hadn't he gone to the young Norwegian's room earlier?

The killer was incredibly bold. He'd run the highest level of risk each time he'd committed a crime, right from the first, absurdly complicated murder up to this attempt on Carin Nolan's life in her own room—under the eyes, so to speak, of those who should have been protecting her. If the murderer had climbed in through Novarreno's window, he'd have had to come through the door this time. He could not, therefore, have come from anywhere but the corridor. And the corridor was guarded by an officer, at certain points two or three—not to mention Sani and De Vincenzi, who'd walked down it and stopped in it at least twice during the night. It was not possible for the man to have come from below or from the third floor. Cruni was upstairs, and the lobby downstairs was being guarded by too many eyes for anyone to have gone past unobserved.

De Vincenzi set about searching Carin Nolan's room carefully. Sani, in the grip of superstitious terror, waited at the door and watched him. In his view, everything that was happening came back to the supernatural, the diabolical. And though at first he'd laughed at De Vincenzi for taking that anonymous letter seriously, now he couldn't stop repeating the banal, theatrical phrase: *the devil is grinning from every corner*.

De Vincenzi hadn't dared to remove the scissors from Carin Nolan's wound. Should he call the usual doctor, who would just be settling down at that hour after a night awake, with the changeover imminent? He preferred to phone the Maggiore Hospital himself, and had them send a stretcher urgently. He explained the situation, pleading with the paramedics to be ready when they arrived at the injured woman's side. So Carin Nolan was laid on the stretcher with the scissors still sticking out of her chest. De Vincenzi had studied them: a pair of large steel scissors, no doubt long and sharp. In any case, the young woman was alive—De Vincenzi was assured of this by the strong and rather accelerated beating of her pulse and heart. She had lost a lot of blood. Not enough to justify her prolonged state of unconsciousness—someone must have administered a narcotic to her as they had to Douglas. De Vincenzi was looking for signs of drugs, but he didn't find any. There was only one beaker on the shelf above the sink, and it hadn't been used: it was perfectly dry, with a faint smell of toothpaste and two toothbrushes in it. An injection, then, or a cotton-wool ball soaked with ether? Even with the window shut tight, there weren't any suspicious smells. De Vincenzi stood in the middle of the room, talking to himself.

"Nothing."

"It's diabolical," Sani said slowly.

"Diabolical?" The inspector was sceptical.

"Can you *imagine* who the killer might be? How he managed to get into the room with the officer never moving from the corridor?"

"Do you actually believe he never stirred? That he never went to sleep, not even for a short time, enough to allow the killer some freedom of movement?"

Sani impulsively turned in order to call the officer but De Vincenzi stopped him.

"No. There's no point. Let's try not to lose another minute, and act only where necessary. How do you think that poor man will answer? Even if he denies it in good faith, what conclusion can you draw? The killer's work is tangible, plain to see—it's staring us in the face. Can that officer's statement negate the fact? Clearly not. So, since it's not possible, and it's unreasonable to think that the killer made himself invisible or passed through these walls, we have to admit that he crossed over the threshold and walked through the corridor twice, the first time to enter the room and the second to leave it."

"But," Sani objected, "I never left the landing, or if I did I went down to the lobby or the dining room... I went up the small staircase to the third floor. So I was always within range of the criminal's actions. And I'm on the alert, I am! How is it possible that I never saw him?"

"There are several objections to your statement, and I'll make them, since I consider it necessary to discuss the situation before taking action. One false step, one ill-timed action could now mean the killer goes unpunished."

"What do you mean?"

"You'll see."

De Vincenzi sat down. He took the hotel plan with the names of the guests written on it from his pocket and studied it for a minute or two.

"Listen. You'll need to follow my instructions to the letter. How many officers are there in the hotel?"

"Four of them—you know that—plus Cruni and the officer guarding the door at the back of the building."

"Four, yes."

De Vincenzi was still looking at the plan in his hands. Sani saw his finger and lips moving as he counted.

"Four officers… thirteen people on this floor, plus a body. Four people on the third floor, plus another body. Downstairs, the manager, his wife, the two maids, the factotum and the four card-players. That's not all—the two Flemingtons in the blue parlour and the porter sleeping somewhere. Too many people."

"And too many bodies," Sani exclaimed.

"Indeed. But they won't be giving us any more trouble." He was growing cynical. He'd overcome his momentary depression and completely recovered his mental lucidity, as well as his cold, implacable determination. The battle had become horrifying and he was facing it determined not to spare any effort—or himself.

"So listen to me. First of all, go to the end of this corridor. The hunchback, Bardi, is in Room 19. Make sure he's still there and is still alive. Then go to Room 21, where there are two rooms, one inside the other, a sort of mini-apartment. You'll find a certain Belloni there with his wife and daughter; he's a cashier at Local Credit. It's highly likely that they're sleeping, but open their door as well, look at them, examine them, count them and then ask them to excuse what you're doing and lock their door. Put the key in your pocket. Understood?"

Sani nodded and De Vincenzi watched as he went off. He stayed where he was, waiting and studying the locked doors one by one. Sani returned with the key in his hand.

"You only told me to lock Room 21, right? Why not Bardi's room?"

"What was Bardi doing?" De Vincenzi asked, lowering his voice almost to a whisper.

Sani did the same. "He seemed to be sleeping. He wouldn't even have known I'd come in."

"Did he have the light on?"

"Yes."

"And did you turn it off?"

"No."

"Good. Come with me and go carefully."

He went back up the corridor to Room 10, next to the empty room of Carin Nolan. He opened it, turned on the light and went in. A man, evidently sleeping and suddenly awakened, sat up in the bed, his eyes wide open. A full face with bovine eyes and tumid lips. His sparse, badly tinted hair stuck out every which way on his head.

"What is it?" he managed to ask in a strangled voice.

"Don't be frightened. Nothing bad for you, other than the bother of having to go down to the dining room. I need all the hotel guests together."

"But why? I'm Donato Desatta, owner of the Orfeo. What do I have to do with the hanged Englishman?"

"It's precisely because you don't have anything to do with it—and I'm sure of that—that I'm asking you to go down to the dining room. I'm asking you, naturally, as a favour."

The man slipped his legs out from under the sheets. He put on some red and blue striped flannel pyjamas. He looked for his slippers but couldn't find them. De Vincenzi put them by his feet. He stood up, pulling the ties of his bottoms over his prominent paunch.

"I have to get dressed," he mumbled, putting a hand through his hair.

"It's not important. You need to hurry. Look, if you want, just put your overcoat over your pyjamas."

"But to go down like this, in the midst of all those people…"

De Vincenzi held out his coat to him, helped him put it on and pushed him towards the door. He called out softly to the officer on duty in the corridor.

"Take him downstairs," he ordered. "Put him with the manager and all the others you'll find in the billiard room—and stay with them. I'll have other people sent down to you. You can let them sleep… gamble… chatter… But make absolutely sure that none of them leaves. Do you understand?"

A few minutes later, he sat in the chair Sani had been sleeping in.

"Come here and let's talk—it'll clear our thoughts. Get a chair for yourself."

Sani was convinced that that was what he needed.

"What were you saying a little while ago? That it wouldn't have been possible for the murderer to have come upstairs and gone down this corridor without being seen by you or the officer? You admit, however, to having wandered from the corridor into the rooms, from this landing to the dining room, from there to the third floor. Not to mention that when I went downstairs last time and passed this way, you were sleeping and didn't even notice me."

Sani looked sheepish.

"Let me continue. It doesn't matter in the least that you were sleeping, and I'll convince you of that shortly. Let's get to the officer. Even if he fell asleep from time to time, as I believe he did, he doubtless wasn't sleeping deeply or for a long time. Given the circumstances, which are certain, one cannot suppose that the person who harmed Carin Nolan—for now let's stick to this last attempt—came in from the outside, nor that he engaged in acrobatics to reach the room, nor did he, after all, have much ground to cover. He would have encountered *too many obstacles*. Do you follow me? Even if he managed to avoid you, he couldn't have avoided the officer, and vice versa; if he came from the third floor, Cruni would have seen him; and if he came from downstairs, he'd have gone by the other two officers in the lobby."

"That's right. But you're forgetting the service stairway, which connects the billiard room with the other part of the corridor. It opens in the corner between Room 22, which is empty, and 21, which is Belloni's mini-apartment. I saw it just now."

"I haven't forgotten it. I have it in mind, as a matter of fact, and I actually believe it played its part in the first crime, yesterday—the murder of Douglas Layng. But it wouldn't have been used last night. And the nature of the problem remains the same, even if we suppose—*mistakenly*, as you'll see—that the murderer used it to get to young Layng's room. All the same, he would only have had to consider the officer in the corner of the corridor, and could have taken advantage of a brief nap or a moment away. That's indisputable, don't you agree?"

"Yes. So this shows that—"

"Hold on—this doesn't show a thing yet, or not enough. And it doesn't give us the name of the killer."

Once again he drew the room plan from his pocket and showed it to Sani. "Let's look at the people who were on this floor when Giorgio Novarreno was killed and Carin Nolan was attacked. In Room 1, Bice Toffoloni, the wife of Agresti; in 2, Stella Essington; in 3, Pompeo Besesti; in Room 7, Nicola Al Righetti. In 8—"

"—the woman with all the little curlers." Sani finished his sentence for him and laughed. His laugh served above all to relieve some of their tension.

"Yes, her. In Room 10, Donato Desatta; in 12, Mary Alton Vendramini; in 19, Stefano Bardi, and finally, in 21, the Belloni family. Let's stick to those people for a moment. My assessment of people and facts may be arbitrary, but I don't think it's wrong, and I would eliminate Toffoloni, Vittoria Jumeta Zogheb, Donato Desatta, the Belloni family and the maids from the list of possible suspects."

"Is that why you had me lock the door on the Belloni family and take the others downstairs?"

"To keep them out of the way and give us free rein shortly."

"So you think that—"

"Why do you want me to have a theory?"

"What are you going to do?"

"Wait, and while we're waiting, we can calmly continue our reflections. If you add the two from the third floor, Carlo Da Como and Vilfredo Engel, and the two English people who arrived last night—"

"Those two couldn't have budged from the blue parlour."

"Of course not. But I was saying that, along with the people I left in their rooms on this floor, everyone involved in this drama is accounted for."

"The men in there—" and Sani pointed to the door to the

corridor "—there are only three left: Pompeo Besesti, Nicola Al Righetti and Bardi, the hunchback."

"Right. But Besesti couldn't have killed Novarreno, because I was with him in his room when the murder was committed. And moreover, Stefano Bardi could not have plunged the scissors into Carin Nolan's chest for the same reason. There's no one left, then, apart from Al Righetti."

"And you saw him. He's from Chicago!"

"Yes. But not one of those I questioned seemed to know of his existence. Only Bardi spoke of him as a persistent—and dangerous—suitor of Carin Nolan. He also mentioned a certain episode involving the offer of cocaine, which was not accepted. But that poor thing, the hunchback, is in love with the young Norwegian, and with his hypersensitivity he may have exaggerated quite a bit. He could also have been mistaken when he told me that Al Righetti was a friend of Da Como and lived with him in London."

"In any case…"

"In any case, the American is thirty-four, and could be Donald Lessinger's son, and could have carried out the three crimes for revenge. You won't be able to understand all of this, because you don't know the story of Major Alton, but I do. See? *All*, or *almost all* the facts needed to explain the mystery—however confused—are to be found there, in my brain. However, it's still inscrutable to me. I can't make sense of them, can't find the links. You know how certain chemicals work in special solutions? All the acids, or sulphides—or whatever the devil they may be, since I can no longer remember what little chemistry I learnt in school—unite in a vessel… But anyway, I know that even when all the ingredients necessary to create the desired precipitate have been assembled in the vessel, nothing

169

happens unless electricity is passed through it to create sparks. The same thing is going on in my head. Everything is there, but I'm not getting any result. The spark is missing."

He fell silent, looking into the emptiness surrounding him, then shook himself and smiled at Sani. Standing up to straighten his legs, he put both hands in his pockets and immediately pulled one out. He moved it so that something glinted in his palm.

"What is that?"

"Half a cufflink, which I found in the built-in wardrobe on the third floor."

"Where the body was hanging?"

"That's it." He put the little gold disc back in his pocket. "Al Righetti… an American who was in London and met Carlo Da Como there and knew his hotel, where people gambled and smoked opium. But he was downstairs eating in the billiard room when Bardi came down shouting that he'd seen the hanged man. And he has an alibi. If I take things at face value, I have to admit that he couldn't have carried out the crime, unless he had an accomplice charged with preparing the macabre scene. But it's unlikely." He passed his hand over his face. "I feel I'm getting closer and closer to the answer, but I can't seem to see what steps I should be taking to find it. Do you know what I mean?"

The two men turned to see Cruni coming up the main staircase.

"Sir, everyone is gathered in the billiard room. They seem like the survivors of a fire, with those two women in their night-gowns and the man in pyjamas. They're so tired and frightened that they don't even have the strength to protest."

"What are they doing?"

"They're just there. The four *scopone* players are continuing their game."

"So then, what do you want?"

"It's almost seven-thirty, sir. Do you want me to go and get Bernasconi?"

"Ah, yes! Go, and be quick about it. He's the old owner of the hotel," De Vincenzi explained to Sani, "and I need to find out a few things." He called Cruni back from the foot of one flight of stairs. "Who's guarding them downstairs?"

"Two men in the dining room who are also watching the door to the billiard room."

"Well done. What about the service stairway that goes from the billiard room to the first floor?"

With a sly wink the sergeant replied, "I've thought about that, sir. There's a bar with a padlock on that door. I shut it and I have the key with me."

"Thank goodness. Go—and come back quickly."

At that moment the telephone rang. Sani ran downstairs.

"It was the hospital. The Norwegian girl is in a very serious condition, but the head physician, who telephoned, hopes to save her. I asked him if it would be possible to question her and he asked me if I was mad. It'll be at least four or five days before she can speak."

"Of course. And who was hoping to get anything out of her?"

He looked at his watch. It was seven-thirty, just as Cruni had said. A dull grey light shone through the huge window on the landing, the first glimmer of dawn sneaking past the thick curtain of rain which continued to fall relentlessly. Before long the hotel would come to life… He shook himself and jumped at the sound of another bell. It was the door at the entrance. Sani went down. De Vincenzi heard him open the little window

171

in the door, speak quietly to someone, then turn. The sound of a metallic clunk on the floor rose up to him.

"It was the milkman. The parade of suppliers is starting."

In other words, Sani too was thinking that they couldn't go on as they were.

"You stay here. But be careful."

"Eh, for sure," murmured the deputy inspector. He would have preferred not to receive those orders. He looked down the corridor with all the doors opening onto it. There was a body there...

"I'm going down to the blue room. I'm going to have everyone still locked in their rooms come down there one by one. I'll periodically send an officer up to you with the name of the person to send down written on a sheet of paper from my notebook. I want you personally to go and get them. But first I have to have a longish interview with the English couple."

"What if—something happens?"

De Vincenzi looked at Sani and put a hand on his shoulder.

"You're a bit tired yourself, aren't you? Don't give up! I honestly believe everything will be over quite soon." He went downstairs.

Sani watched him go, and then shook his head sadly. It was more than tiredness. He couldn't put up with any more. He took a chair and placed it at the beginning of the corridor. At least that way no one would go by without his seeing him and being able to stop him. But not even that precaution—which seemed absolutely necessary to Sani—could stop the fatal course of events. Nor did it.

17

The Flemington couple were sleeping when De Vincenzi went into the blue room. The lamp was still on.

Mrs Flemington was breathing unevenly and shifting fitfully. Her husband, in shirtsleeves and without collar or tie, had slumped over the table where his head lay, shattered by tiredness and drinking. Before him, a black revolver and the square bottle of whisky made two marks on the red velvet cloth. His glass lay overturned not far away, a bit of liquor spilt from it and smearing the carpet. Nothing in the room had been moved. The pile of luggage reached right up to the window. It was cold in there. Left unattended, the central heating boiler must have cooled down and the room, level with the inner courtyard, had absorbed all the damp from the pouring rain.

De Vincenzi noisily shifted a chair, coughed and took a few steps around the room. He left the door open so he could call an officer if necessary. In the lobby, the officer paced back and forth to keep warm, his steps resounding on the stone floor.

All at once, Mrs Flemington turned on her side and groaned. Her husband slowly raised his head, placed an elbow on the table and tried to get comfortable enough to go back to sleep. He blinked and moaned.

"Flemington!"

He looked at the inspector without recognizing him. His eyes were dark and troubled, he'd paled and his cheeks were drooping. The lines around his mouth were deeper and threw his purplish lips and his prominent and commanding nose into relief.

"What's going on? What do you want?" He looked around, and when he saw his wife his memory began to return. "Ah…" He grabbed the revolver, keeping it covered with his large hand, on the small finger of which sparkled a diamond. He then laughed and withdrew his hand. His laugh had recovered its grating tone and his expression cleared instantly. "Who've they killed now! You're not coming to tell me that some other Novar—, Bonar—, —ceno… another bizarre name of someone I don't know… or perhaps I'll discover I'm in some nuthouse."

"Stop laughing, please, Mr Flemington."

He stopped and waited.

"The moment has come for you to talk. Tell me everything. Vilfredo Engel has told me about Major Alton and his brother. Pompeo Besesti has also started down the confessional path. Was he the fifth person you wrote to and asked to come here?"

"Indeed."

"Then you'll need to tell me *everything you know* and acquaint me with the terms of the will."

"What about Julius Lessinger? What are you doing with him? Have you found him? Who else has been killed—of these five?"

"Someone tried to kill Carin Nolan, but she'll live."

"What about you? What have you done?"

"I'm carrying out my duty, Flemington. And in order to do so, I must insist that you speak."

"Do you think what I have to say will help you stop the murderer? The heirs, or at least, the heirs presumptive… there are five, and so far he's killed only two. It's not a lot." He emphasized this with one of his peculiar laughs. "We're still

174

here, my wife and I... Lessinger won't do things by half. He wrote that to me."

De Vincenzi jumped. So Julius Lessinger actually existed? Was he really the one De Vincenzi had to arrest?

"I've taken all the precautions I possibly could, and as it happens nothing has threatened you and Mrs Flemington before now. Show me what Julius Lessinger wrote to you."

Flemington got up and moved the chair from the table. For several moments he remained standing, as if trying to get his balance. When he moved, however, he wasn't unsteady. He took his jacket from the back of the chair and put it on. Then he drew a bunch of keys from his trouser pocket. He went to the suitcases and set the smallest one, in black leather, on a nearby chair and opened it. Every movement was slow and studied, and he hesitated for a moment before each one. Without a doubt, the man had great control over himself, but he must still be feeling numb with alcohol. He turned back to the table and sat down. In his hand was an envelope. He put it down in front of him and then pushed it across the table to De Vincenzi. The letter bore the address of George Flemington in Lincoln's Inn Fields and was postmarked Hamburg. It was in English, and the whole of it was typewritten, even the signature.

> The person who killed my father and my sisters has always escaped my revenge. But it will fall on those who expect to divide the spoils. Even the innocent will pay for the guilt of their fathers. I'll get them when they're ready to reach for the blood money. Everything will happen in the course of twenty-four hours, and you'll be with them. A mother will fall on the body of her son. A brother will

atone for the guilt of his brother. They'll have three roses on their tombs.

JULIUS LESSINGER

De Vincenzi slowly folded the piece of paper and put it back in the envelope. He heard Mrs Flemington's quiet moaning; having woken up, she was now crying. Flemington turned towards the sofa and said in a harsh voice, "Diana! It's useless crying."

De Vincenzi saw the woman hurry to dry her eyes as she sat up on the sofa, recomposing herself and trying to reassume her proud, dignified air.

"Mr Flemington, everything I learnt from the others allows me to understand this letter almost entirely. But I still don't know what sort of ties bound you to Harry Alton. Would you describe them for me?"

"Are you trying to initiate proceedings against the dead?"

"I'm only trying to understand the intentions of those who are still alive. Tell me everything you know about Julius Lessinger."

"He is Donald's son."

"Who told him how his father and sisters were killed?"

"I don't know."

"Who could have told him about the death of Major Alton, and above all, about the meeting between the heirs in this hotel? The allusion to the three roses is significant. How could Julius Lessinger have known? What do *you* know about Julius Lessinger?"

"I was in Sydney in 1915."

"Were you in business with Alton?"

"Not exactly. In fact, I wasn't at all. But I was the major's legal consultant and I assisted him."

"In a serious trial?"

"If you are interested, I'll explain. But I'd reiterate that this seems the wrong moment to reconstruct the entire life of a dead man."

"So let's say it was a trial for coastal trading, in other words supplying submarines on the high seas."

Flemington interrupted him, and for the first time his voice betrayed his anxiety. "Did Scotland Yard send you a wire?"

A smile from De Vincenzi. It was in his interest for the other man to believe it.

"It's not important, Mr Flemington. That's not what matters. Go on. You knew Julius Lessinger in Sydney?"

"Someone spoke to me about him, someone who'd met him."

"Pompeo Besesti."

"You know that too?"

"I guessed it."

"Yes, it was Besesti who spoke to me about him, and who first revealed to Alton that Lessinger's son knew about how his father had been killed."

"And Besesti thus became Alton's partner," De Vincenzi said, as if to himself.

The lawyer could not contain a look of stupefaction.

"All this deduction is your work?"

"Easy! Besesti told you he'd known Julius Lessinger personally?"

"He did."

Exactly. How could he not have known him? The bankrupt from Buenos Aires had had dealings with Lessinger, learnt the story of the four murders and the box of diamonds and left for Australia in search of Alton. When he found him, the game had been easy. He became the major's business partner and kept him under the thumb of his secret. And that's how the Bank of Pure Metals had been founded—with a capital deposit of ten million. All this was simple to reconstruct. It was, however, more difficult to explain why Julius Lessinger, knowing the tragic story and determined to revenge himself, had not himself gone to Australia—and had let Harry Alton die a peaceful and natural death only to enact his revenge on the innocent in this horrifying manner. It was unthinkable that he had not traced the major's footsteps, given that he was now demonstrating perfect knowledge of everything about him, including the story of the three roses, the existence of Alton's son, who bore a name which wasn't his father's, even the ties that bound Alton to the Flemington couple. But what, in the end, were those ties? Was it possible that Flemington had always acted and continued to this day to act for the major—even at the risk of his own life? *My wife held Douglas Layng on her lap as a baby...*

De Vincenzi looked at the woman. She was still sitting up straight in her chair, immobile, staring at her husband, as if to draw from him the strength required for her impassivity, which after all was only superficial. The silence persisted, cold and heavy. Slowly, slowly the shadows lifted, while others blew in thick behind them. Nothing De Vincenzi had managed to discover was helping him to proceed towards a solution to the problem. The revelations were jumbling up in his head, superimposing themselves on one another in no discernible order. The spark was missing.

"So Pompeo Besesti must be able to recognize Julius Lessinger." He paused. The Flemingtons stayed seated, unmoving.

"You set today as the day for the reading of Harry Alton's will, is that right?"

The lawyer nodded in agreement.

"Good. I'm going to have the people you convened come in here."

"Not all of them," sneered Flemington.

"Not all," the inspector repeated, and he then became brusque. "Mr Flemington, do you know the terms of the will?"

"No. Alton sent it to me in a sealed envelope a couple of months ago, when the doctor told him there was no hope. He absolutely prohibited me from opening it until after his death and in the presence of those five people he nominated... *those five people and the three porcelain dolls*. That was his precise wish."

"The third doll must be in Carin Nolan's room. But why in *this* hotel?"

Surprised by the question, Flemington hesitated.

"Don't tell me you can't explain it, because the major himself stated in the letter to his wife, which I have here, that you know very well about this hotel."

"It was here that Harry Alton was married."

"For that reason alone?"

"When he decided to marry Miss Mary Vendramini, the major agreed to meet his future wife in Milan and this was where they met up."

"So you're saying that it was Mrs Alton who chose this hotel?"

"She waited here in any event for the major's arrival."

"And you?"

"I... was called by Sir Alton to be one of the witnesses at the marriage."

"And the other witness?"

"The lady ought to have chosen one, but she refused. The pastor took it upon himself to find an English person passing through or else living in Milan who would perform that favour. It was an older man whose name I don't remember."

"You see no other reason that might have induced the major to choose this place as the meeting point for his heirs?"

"Alton had his irrational fears and superstitions. The fact that he was married here could have been enough for him to have suggested it."

De Vincenzi quickly wrote down a name at the top of a page in his notebook and went to the door. He gave the paper to the officer in the lobby and then returned to the table.

"Was it Lessinger's letter that made you fear for the life of young Douglas Layng?"

"Yes."

"Why had Layng already been in Milan for a month?"

Flemington glanced at his wife. "The boy wanted to visit Italy and he was taking advantage of the fact that he had to come here anyway."

"Therefore, Douglas Layng knew before the major died that *he would have to come to this hotel to hear the reading of his father's will*. Who told him?"

The lawyer bit his lip.

"I did," he said reluctantly.

"Why?"

"It wasn't a secret."

"Did you let anyone else know?"

"No, but at the station, where my wife and I went to see Douglas off, he told me he'd spoken to Mrs Mary Alton about the reason for his departure."

"So the boy knew his father's wife?"

"He couldn't *not* know her, since when the major married her he was already grown up."

"Why didn't Alton give his name to his son?"

Another brief hesitation.

180

"Alton abandoned Layng's mother, leaving her alone with the baby. She gave her son her maiden name."

"Where is that woman now?"

"She married another man."

"It was in Australia, of course, that Alton met her?"

"Yes."

"Did Alton see her again later?"

"Yes."

"Her husband didn't know about him?"

"No."

The officer opened the door to let in Mary Alton Vendramini. Flemington rose. The widow wore an open expression, with her pure profile under that great mass of golden hair. She was so fragile...

"Pardon me, Signora, for having asked you to come down." De Vincenzi then turned to Flemington and continued in English: "The lawyer, Flemington, will shortly read your husband's will." He pulled up a chair for her. She sat down, nodding a greeting to Mrs Flemington, who hadn't taken her eyes off her from the moment she'd come in and was resting, dignified.

"You didn't bring the doll with you, Signora?"

She looked at him, stunned.

"The doll also needs to be here for the reading of the will. Major Alton stipulated that as an essential condition."

"If it's really necessary," Mary Alton murmured, and she made as if to get up.

"Not now. I'll ask you to go and get it before the reading begins."

De Vincenzi remained standing. He paused very briefly before beginning to question the woman in a cold voice, still in English so that the Flemingtons could understand.

181

"Why, Mrs Alton, did you deny knowing Douglas Layng?"

Mary's eyes flashed.

"Because it wasn't necessary for me to tell you!"

"But it was also true that you knew him! Did he trust you?"

"We were friends."

"And he told you about this meeting that would take place at the Three Roses?"

"He told me he was coming to Milan and that he'd be staying at this hotel. In any case, my husband's letter was sufficiently clear for me."

"But you knew from Douglas Layng even before you received that letter?"

"Maybe."

"Knowing the boy, and as the friends you say you were, why were you not upset? Why didn't you show the least sign of concern when you heard about his tragic death?" But he gave her no time to respond. "And why, from the moment that you arrived in Milan yesterday morning, have you not looked for him? You didn't let him know you were coming?"

She answered with innocent simplicity.

"I knew Julius Lessinger might be here, and I knew... that all of us were in danger. It occurred to me that it wouldn't have done the young man any good to be seen with me."

"But after his death?"

"Do you know exactly what happened in here, from the moment that man came screaming into the dining room? Everyone panicked! For my part, I knew that the death of Douglas was only *the first*, and it was something even more: it was terrifying. Why should I talk? To what end? I could do nothing but wait—for my turn."

"Did you know Carin Nolan?"

"I knew who she was and I'd spoken to her a couple of times. Carin Nolan didn't live in London."

"Mr Flemington, how do you explain the fact that Carin Nolan also came to Milan—to this hotel—at almost the same time as Douglas Layng?"

Flemington answered bluntly.

"Same reason as for the boy. And besides, Douglas and Carin were friends."

It wasn't a very convincing reply, but De Vincenzi turned again to the widow.

"Who told you the story of the Vaal crocodiles, Mrs Alton?"

"It was Harry. At a time when he felt Lessinger was getting closer…"

"In London?"

"Yes."

"And he didn't want to take the doll away from you? Didn't he want to destroy it?"

"Why would he have done that?"

"For the same reason he asked Engel to give him a similar doll that had belonged to his brother."

"Yes, Harry asked me for the doll. But I was the one who didn't want to give it to him, and I told him I'd lost it. A few years later, though, when it seemed he was no longer worried about Lessinger's threat, I confessed to him that I'd lied, and told him I… was fond of the doll and that it would be painful for me if he took it away."

"Did you know of the existence of the other two dolls?"

"Of course."

"What did you do in Milan yesterday, Signora Alton?"

"Oh, nothing in particular. I was in my room. I took a walk around the city."

"What time?"

"I went out after lunch and came back around six."

The doorbell rang and the front door opened. Voices. The officer came back into the lobby accompanied by two men with a stretcher. They went out and came in again, carrying in a second stretcher. De Vincenzi heard the men shuffling around and the dull sound of the stretchers being set down.

"One moment!" he said, and he left the blue room.

They had come to take the bodies to the Monumentale cemetery. One of the men went up to De Vincenzi and gave him a paper.

"It's the authorization from the investigating magistrate. He'll be here shortly."

"Go to the third floor first; then you can take the one from the first floor."

The officer took the two soldiers with the stretcher upstairs. De Vincenzi turned round quickly. Mrs Flemington had appeared at the door of the blue room, and behind her was her husband. She stood straight and proud, yet she was as stiff and pale as a candle. She stared at the stretchers, her eyes wide.

De Vincenzi's first move was to run and push her back into the room. But she stayed there, waiting. The minutes were interminable. Mr Flemington kept silent behind his wife, but he was clearly worried. He heard steps on the stairs, slow and measured. They stopped. Began again...

At the top of the stairs: the head of the first soldier, the stretcher, the second soldier. More steps, one for each stair, measured, equal. They got to the lobby. The dull thud of the stretcher set on the floor.

A white face and bare shoulder slipped out from under the sheet. A sharp, lacerating scream echoed through the lobby.

Diana Flemington fell to her knees over the body of Douglas Layng. Neither her husband nor De Vincenzi made a move. The lawyer looked at the inspector and for the first time his eyes were human, soft and dismayed.

18

Mrs Flemington was helped to the sofa in the blue room by her husband and De Vincenzi, who had to persuade her with gentle force. Her husband stood up straight beside her.

De Vincenzi went over to Mary Alton, who hadn't budged from her chair. The widow gazed at him with her velvety, violet eyes, so dark, clear and innocent. Every time he looked at her, De Vincenzi had the same impression as the first time he'd seen her: gentle and peaceful. He wished he could trust this woman; her purity worked on him like a nepenthe, reconciling him with his fellow man and with life. Even in the midst of all this moral filth, this horrendous procession of bodies, the young woman remained pure, white and innocent as the Lamb of God.

"Mrs Alton," he said with unwitting gentleness, "you must now go and get the porcelain doll. I'd like you to bring the one that belonged to Carin Nolan as well, which you'll surely find in her room. It's number 9, at the beginning of the other part of the corridor."

Mary stood up. She looked at De Vincenzi. "Aren't the others who should be present at the reading of the will going to come down?"

Flemington's grating voice rose from behind De Vincenzi, at the back of the room. "They'll come down, Mrs Alton." And he laughed in that sarcastic way of his.

"Why couldn't I go when all the others have got here?"

"Sit down, please," De Vincenzi ordered.

Was the woman afraid of going upstairs? Did she think she'd be safer when *all* the heirs—apart from the dead and the wounded Carin—were gathered together in that room? Without waiting for him to repeat his words, Mary sat down and put her hands in her lap, her blond head tilted towards her shoulder. She seemed relaxed, but also to be waiting for something resignedly. De Vincenzi wrote another name in his notebook and handed the page to his officer to give to Sani.

"Mrs Flemington—" He paused.

The woman grew still paler. Her husband took a step towards her as if to defend her.

"Mrs Flemington," De Vincenzi repeated respectfully and courteously, "would you mind telling me your maiden name?"

"Layng," replied the woman in a firm voice. Immediately she threw a beseeching look at her husband.

Flemington nodded in consent and when he turned back to the inspector he said confidentially, "Miss Layng, and she was born in Australia."

"Thank you." De Vincenzi turned on his heel and made for the door. He wanted the lawyer to understand that there was nothing more to say on the subject, and that he attached no importance to Mrs Flemington's having been Harry Alton's lover and the mother of Douglas Layng.

He waited at the door. When Pompeo Besesti arrived, he moved out of the way.

"Come in!"

The owner of the Bank of Pure Metals had lost all his pride. His face, usually round and ruddy, was now pale and drawn, and his golden beard was no longer impeccably tidy. His hair was dishevelled and his blue eyes were swimming in terror and confusion. He'd come down without his fur coat, and since his tie had shifted and almost entirely come out of his waistcoat, the huge diamond on it was twirling and throwing its glorious rays around. When he saw Flemington, he perked up somewhat.

"Mr Flemington!" and he ran towards him as if seeking protection. "Ah, Mr Flemington!"

The lawyer sneered in his typical way.

"Mr Besesti! *Your* Lessinger has finally made himself known."

The phrase was a body blow, and Besesti wavered and stopped mid-step.

"What are you saying? What in the world are you saying?"

"Didn't he swear to revenge himself, Julius Lessinger? Wasn't it you he announced it to? Wasn't it you who took the news to Harry? Happy news, which from that moment made his existence truly pleasant!"

"But it can't be him. It can't be Lessinger!"

"Then who? Who could have killed Douglas? Who could have wished the death of Carin Nolan?"

"Miss Nolan—killed?" The question came as a strangled scream.

"That's right, Miss Nolan. If he didn't kill her, it was close."

"Oh!" He waved his arms in the air and then brought them to his throat, as if he were about to suffocate.

De Vincenzi had gone over to the window where he was almost hidden by the curtain, and stood listening to the two men, staring at them and not missing a move. Signora Alton looked at Besesti with curiosity, as if asking herself what this new character had to do with anything. But only for an instant before she became listless again, a condition that isolated her, rendering her almost non-existent.

Flemington laughed. De Vincenzi told himself that the nightmare would continue for as long as he had to keep hearing that laugh.

"And now, look over there at the table. There's the letter Lessinger wrote to me!"

"To you? Lessinger?" He grabbed the piece of paper and quickly scanned it. He began rereading from the top. His terror was making him weak and jerky. He looked around desperately for some escape, and found none. "No! No!"

He was spluttering. Just then he saw the whisky bottle and the upturned glass. He grabbed the bottle with one hand, the glass with the other and poured the liquor until it was overflowing. He drank it down in one, and was revived by the alcohol. Taking his silk handkerchief out of his breast pocket, he wiped his mouth, then adjusted his tie. He touched his diamond.

"It's very strange!"

De Vincenzi came forward. "Why is it so strange, Signor Besesti?" He stared at Besesti, who returned his gaze in wonderment, surely noticing the inspector only then.

"I left Lessinger in America."

"What year?"

"In '13, I think. '13."

"You haven't come across him since then?"

"Not once."

"Would you recognize him if you saw him?"

Once more, Besesti acted as if there were a ghost in front of him. He threw his hands out in defence.

"It's not possible!"

"But actually, Mr Besesti, why don't you want to admit that Lessinger wanted to take his revenge, since you knew that better than anyone else? Why shouldn't he be in Milan, if he wrote that letter to Mr Flemington from Hamburg? And why not him—*and only him*—if Layng's body was hung from a rope, as they did to Donald Lessinger? After Douglas, Carin Nolan... Dick Nolan's niece. The boy's body was put upstairs *where Vilfredo Engel would have to see it*! Isn't all of this enough to indicate that Lessinger is the murderer—*and that it could only be him*? Why don't you believe it? Why? Why?"

De Vincenzi hammered out the words. He advanced towards Besesti as he spoke, peering into the depths of his eyes. But madness was the only thing he saw burning in them.

"But no! No! It's impossible!"

"Who else could it have been then?"

This obvious question, laying out a simple problem which was unavoidable and logical after his obstinate denial, seemed to recall him to reason. The change was visible. All his features loosened, as if they'd relaxed. He crinkled his forehead and set his mouth, making a considerable effort to ponder the question, to concentrate.

"Who? Who can it have been?"

"*And who is it*, still here in this hotel... and who will keep killing, right to the end, if we don't stop him?"

Besesti held on to the table and stood up straight, apparently recovering something of his self-confidence.

"How should I know? You're the one who's supposed to find him!"

"Yet you, Besesti, don't allow that it could be Lessinger! What reasons do you have for not believing it's him? That's what I want to know."

Flemington, too, had come closer in order to watch Besesti. Mrs Flemington's low groans of suffering could be heard.

"I said it wasn't him because I can't imagine how he could have got here. Because I haven't seen him since." He was searching for reasons, panting. It was pitiful to watch him trying to hide behind his quibbling. He seized on a logical point and shouted: "And because he would have killed Harry Alton, first of all. He wouldn't have left him to die a natural death!"

"Who says Harry died a natural death? His illness was a mystery. He knew he was dying and there was no doctor who could save him. Why? No one has ever said what Harry died of. He could have been poisoned."

All of them shivered. Diana Flemington moaned desperately. De Vincenzi rushed towards the widow. It was she who had spoken in her melodious voice. The look on her face was unchanged and her cheeks remained pale. Flemington instinctively reached out and grasped the revolver on the table. Besesti drew his right hand across his forehead, sliding it right down to his cheek. He was trying to understand. He looked back and forth. The pent-up silence—anxious, terrified—continued for only moments, but it seemed an eternity.

"It's true, Signora. No one knows how your husband died."

De Vincenzi had turned cold again.

"However, before long we'll know at least if Lessinger is really here." He called his officer and whispered in his ear outside the door. The officer ran up the main staircase and De Vincenzi turned back to the blue room. "Let's sit down. The others are coming now."

Flemington wouldn't let go of the revolver. Still gripping it, he went to sit on the sofa beside his wife, whose face was wet with tears; she stopped moaning when she saw him next to her.

The first to enter was Da Como, and behind him, with curved shoulders, lumbered the elephantine Vilfredo Engel. He'd put his overcoat over his pyjamas and was wearing his red slippers. Da Como looked around, smiled and greeted everyone with the sweep of his hand. Engel was puffing and panting. He was pale and his pupils, always small, seemed two bright dots in the middle of the unhealthy swelling of his eyes. His brain must have been foggy with alcohol, but he managed to reach Flemington; he shook his hand and bowed to his wife. Then he sat down, huge and grotesque, on a chair too small for his bulk.

"You sit down too."

Da Como saw a chair near the table. He went to get it and moved it away into the corner. He sat there as if to signal his detachment from everyone else.

"Mr Flemington, you may now read the will."

"This man," the lawyer immediately objected, pointing to Da Como, "was not summoned, so—"

"It doesn't matter!"

"And also missing—"

"Douglas Layng and Carin Nolan. I know."

"Not just those two. The three dolls aren't here."

"You're right!"

De Vincenzi turned to Engel.

"Where have you put yours, Mr Engel?"

"In the second drawer of the dresser," he pronounced in his deep, hoarse voice. "Here's the key." He drew it from his overcoat pocket.

De Vincenzi took it from him, went into the lobby and sent the officer to the third floor to get the doll. He called Cruni, who was sitting on the wicker sofa beside a thin and jaundiced old man with his hand at his mouth, biting his nails.

"Sir, that man is the old owner of this hotel."

"Right," said De Vincenzi. "Go and stand at the door to the blue room and don't take your eyes off the people in there, not even for a moment." He went and sat down in Cruni's place.

"Signor Bernasconi—am I right?"

The little man took his hand from his mouth. "That's me, and I am really angry, my dear inspector. I was in bed! I have nothing more to do with what happens in *my* hotel. It's rented! This is not good manners. Why did you have me come here? I've always been a Swiss subject, and I am entitled to your respect."

"You have every right, my dear Bernasconi. But I need some information."

"And you couldn't wait for it? Does this seem a Christian hour to you, seven in the morning?"

"You were running the hotel yourself in '14?"

"Of course I was. And it was going better than this, I can tell you! I knew how to choose my guests, I did. I'd hardly have taken in—"

"Listen to me," the inspector interrupted brusquely.

Bernasconi brought his hand to his mouth and started biting his nails again.

"Do you remember a young woman with an Italian name and a somewhat older Englishman, Major Harry Alton, who stayed in your hotel that year? The young woman's name was Mary Vendramini."

Bernasconi continued nibbling the ends of his fingers while looking straight at the inspector.

"Do you remember? They got married while they were staying in your hotel. The ceremony was at the Protestant church in Piazza Missori."

He didn't speak, but removed one hand and started stripping the nails from the other.

"Well?"

"Yes, I remember them. She was blonde. He was tall and angular, with thick grey hair. There was another Englishman with them. All three left together."

"Do you remember anything else?"

"What else should I remember?"

"Did the *signora* arrive first?"

"Yes." The little man became nervous and squirmed on the sofa.

"Tell me what you know."

"So much time has passed!"

"But you have a good memory. No! Stop that. You can continue biting your nails in a moment. For now, talk!"

"What manners!" the old man stuttered. Then he talked. "I don't have anything to do with this. Why do you want to know all this from *me*?"

"Tell me. The information is just for me. You don't have to make a statement. I give you my word that you won't be questioned by the investigating magistrate, either."

"Well, that hunchback, Bardi, was also in the hotel. He too could tell you."

So Bardi had been lying when he'd said he didn't know anything or remember anything else about Mary. Because there was undoubtedly something else that he could have told him.

"Fine. I'll question Bardi as well. But you can talk now!"

"That lady had been to this hotel three times before, at regular intervals—starting in 1912, I think, or before."

"Alone?"

"No. A man always arrived at the same time. But they each took a separate room."

"Did they arrive together?"

"Yes. They also ate together."

"Was the man young?"

"More or less her age."

"So—young."

"That's right."

"And the last time she was here—when she married the old man?"

"The other man was here too. Naturally, as soon as the Englishman arrived, the two of them made a show of not knowing each other. But the old man wasn't so dumb. He saw right through people."

"What do you mean?"

"The major asked me about the young man. He wanted me to talk. He put a gold coin in my hand."

"What did you tell him?"

"Me? Nothing. I'm hardly stupid! But he asked the servants, everyone he could. He even bought a watch from the hunchback to make him talk."

"Thank you. That's all for now. I understand." De Vincenzi stood up.

Bernasconi was baffled. He'd got going now and he wanted to continue.

"Well?" he said. "Can I go home?"

"Of course. And thank you."

The old man toddled to the door and slipped into the courtyard.

"Here's the doll, sir."

De Vincenzi took her. Holding her in his hands, he looked at her briefly, noticing that she was an old doll. A bit of the porcelain on her neck had actually peeled off and her cheeks had faded, so that only the two rosettes on them remained vivid.

How many years had this doll *been alive*? The three sisters…
the Vaal crocodiles… Of course! The pink gauze skirt was new.
But Engel's doll was the same as the one that belonged to
Mary—*"it's mine!"*—and had the same pink gauze skirt. Who
had re-dressed them, those two?

He passed Cruni and went back into the blue room. Everyone
shuddered when they saw him with the doll—everyone except
Mary Alton, who said in her melodious voice, "My doll! Did you
go and get it?"

"It's not yours, Mrs Alton."

He took it to Engel, who grabbed it awkwardly with his
enormous hands. Not knowing what else to do with it, he put
it on his lap, its mouth hanging open and its arms out as if it
were drowning.

"Now, Signora, you can go and get *yours*, and also Carin
Nolan's, if you please."

The widow stood up. "I'm going," she said.

She started walking. How fragile she was, and how beautiful!
She didn't have time to leave the room before Cruni stepped
away from the door, and on the threshold appeared a red-
haired woman in green and yellow pyjamas. She was smoking
through a long ivory cigarette-holder. Her eyes were shining, lit
by hundreds of flickering lights. She took the cigarette-holder
from her mouth and twisted her lips in a look of disgust. She
was terribly pale, and there were several russet-coloured marks
on her forehead and neck.

"I've come as well. Didn't you want me here? And yet I'm
meant to be here. Everyone gathered together, eh, for the reading of the will! There's a million pounds to share out. A nice nest
egg! But I'm part of it. He told me so. He told me everything,
he did. I was the only woman he spoke to. A lovely man, and

so young! Did you think I wouldn't find you? I was looking for the inspector, and I've found everyone here. Much better. That way the rest of you will hear me!"

Sani stood behind her, perplexed. He'd been hoping to grab her but hadn't dared.

"I tried to stop her, but she ran ahead of me."

"It's not important," said De Vincenzi. "Come on in."

He was so used to speaking English to those people in the blue room that he had spoken to Stella in English as well.

"So you think I don't understand English? I don't speak it, but I understand it."

She came in. Mary Alton backed away, unobtrusively and with her usual gracefulness. She sat down. Everyone around her kept quiet and looked at the woman in green and yellow pyjamas with dyed red hair, trying in vain to understand how she had suddenly appeared in their midst at that precise moment. Sani and Cruni remained at the door to stop anyone from escaping.

Stella looked for a chair and, seeing one against a wall, went to sit on it, crossing her legs. On her feet were slippers with two large white feather puffs that covered her ankles. De Vincenzi left her no time to reprise her soliloquy.

"Now that you're here, you'll answer my questions."

"Oh, oh, what a tone! Of course I'll answer... if I want to."

"No. You'll answer all the questions I put to you unless you'd prefer to go to San Fedele straightaway."

The woman blanched.

"What are you saying?"

"I'm telling you I'll send you to San Fedele and have them take out the file on Rosetta Carboni."

Stella bit her lip till it bled. She was on the verge of a panic attack, but De Vincenzi put a stop to it.

"Keep quiet and answer me. It's the best thing for you to do at this point. How did you know Douglas Layng didn't die by hanging, but was killed before that?"

"I knew that? Who told you I knew that? I didn't know anything."

The inspector took a step towards the door.

"No!" she shouted immediately. "All of this is vile!"

"When I questioned you for the first time, you yourself said, word for word: *how do you know he didn't die by hanging*? Therefore, you knew it too."

She bent her head, put her cigarette-holder in her mouth and hurriedly blew several puffs of smoke.

"I knew it because I saw him dead in his room."

All of them started, apart from George and Diana Flemington, who didn't understand Italian. Even the widow shivered, and her eyes went dark and shiny like two hard gemstones. Engel's doll slid to the floor.

"What time?"

"It must have been eight at night, or shortly before."

"Why didn't you scream? Why didn't you raise the alarm?"

She answered violently, getting up from her chair. "Because if I had I would have died too!"

"So you saw the murderer, and the murderer saw you?"

The question made her conscious of the full force of her impetuous affirmation. The blood drained completely from her face to her heart; she looked ashen. She went quiet and her eyes widened. The ivory cigarette-holder dropped to the ground with a click.

Stella Essington looked around, saw Sani and Cruni at the door and backed away. Perhaps she hadn't recognized them, or thought they'd block her escape. She let out a sharp, piercing scream, like that of an injured beast. It was a moment of agonizing terror for everyone. Even the English couple jumped to their feet.

De Vincenzi barely made it in time. He grabbed Flemington's wrist and tore the revolver he'd pointed at Stella from his grasp. He put it in his pocket and turned to Stella, who'd backed up against the wall, her eyes bursting from their sockets, her lips pursed, her hands extended in front of her.

"No! No! It's not true! It's not true!"

All hell broke loose as she watched De Vincenzi approach. She crumpled to the ground, muscles twitching, nails dug into her flesh and her teeth gnashing. Sani and De Vincenzi took hold of her and physically carried her out of the room. When they got to the lobby they set her down on the wicker sofa. She was so tense, so rigid, that she slid immediately to the floor, overturning the little table.

"Call a taxi!" De Vincenzi ordered Cruni.

"*Who* is she afraid of?" asked Sani.

"I'll tell you later. Get her to the hospital because as long as she's here, she won't talk."

They put her in the cab and Cruni got in with her.

"Don't leave her bed."

And the taxi took off in the rain, with the woman in yellow and green pyjamas slowly losing consciousness, slumped against the seat.

Cruni lit a cigar stub. It was hours since he'd smoked and he could stand it no longer.

19

As he went back into the lobby with Sani, De Vincenzi murmured, "We're nearing the end, but the most dreadful thing is yet to come."

He went into the blue room, where everyone was still standing. They looked at him in terror, as if expecting him to announce a further catastrophe. He feigned indifference, even smiled.

"Please sit down. Miss Essington is a little deranged. She can't have seen anybody or any killer. The cocaine is giving her hallucinations." He turned to Mary Alton. "We must finish this as soon as possible. I'd like you, Mrs Alton, to go and get the dolls."

The widow was momentarily somewhat perplexed, as if she hadn't understood. She let out a deep sigh and fluttered her eyelashes. De Vincenzi repeated the request. She then nodded and left in a rush. Her quick, light steps could be heard on the staircase—then nothing. The men sat down. Mrs Flemington was so petrified with fear that her husband had to reach out and take her arm, drawing her closer to him.

"Are you perfectly sure, Besesti, *that the killer can't be Lessinger*?"

"Yes. It can't be Julius Lessinger."

"Why not?"

He didn't answer. It was clear he was struggling to swallow, as if his throat had closed up.

"Why not?"

"Because… Julius Lessinger died in Buenos Aries in 1913."

It was such an extraordinary revelation that everyone was struck speechless. The first to recover was the lawyer. He leapt to his feet, threatening Besesti with a raised fist.

"Scoundrel!"

Besesti's head drooped.

"Dastardly blackmailer!"

"Quiet, Flemington!" shouted De Vincenzi.

"He's a scoundrel! He terrorized Harry Alton for five years with the threat of Lessinger's revenge."

"Be quiet now!" The inspector forced him to sit back down.

"It's true," muttered Besesti. "But I didn't talk to the major about Lessinger after—"

"After you convinced him to become your partner in the coastal trading business."

"Yes. I met Julius Lessinger by chance in hospital in Buenos Aires. He had a bed next to mine, and he was very sick—tuberculosis—and he wasn't going to get better. He confided the whole story to me."

"How had he heard it?"

"It seems he'd got Dick Nolan drunk one day and made him talk. He was the one who killed him in battle. He shot him in the back. He didn't kill Alton as well because he wanted to recover the box of diamonds first. Then he got sick and was sent back to Johannesburg. Meanwhile, Alton and Engel had gone to England. What Lessinger was doing in Buenos Aires I've no idea. All I know is that he died in despair, because he wanted to revenge himself on Alton and he'd managed to find out where he was."

"In Sydney?"

"Yes."

"What about you?"

"When Lessinger died, I left for Sydney. My situation in Buenos Aires had become unsustainable."

"And from Lessinger's story you immediately saw a way of recouping your fortune!"

Flemington was still in a state of overexcitement. He was exasperated by Besesti's ugly game with Harry Alton—the pretence that Lessinger was still alive and the blackmail threat—with its consequences for himself and his wife, the mother of Douglas Layng.

"But that letter! Who wrote that letter, then?" Flemington roared, his finger pointing at the table where the letter from Hamburg was still lying.

"The person who wrote it wanted to do what they have done, making everyone believe it was Lessinger," came the calm voice of De Vincenzi. "Mr Besesti, did anyone besides you know about Lessinger's death?"

"I kept quiet with everyone!" He got up. "I swear by Christ I haven't spoken about Julius Lessinger for five years, to Alton or to anyone else. The threats to him did not come from me."

He was sincere. Once he had succeeded with the initial blackmail, and had got rich from it, what point was there in continuing to make use of the secret? After all, it was dangerous enough to send his business partner to the gallows—and their fates were linked. Apparently, someone else who knew the horrifying story of the killings had impersonated Lessinger, taking care to keep Alton's terror on the boil. But why?

And what was the motive for killing Douglas Layng, for having injured and nearly killed Carin Nolan, and for keeping all the other guests under the imminent threat of death?

The deep, harsh voice of Vilfredo Engel sounded strangely troubled. "Whoever the murderer may be, it's one of us."

That he was in the hotel was clear, considering the fact that Stella Essington had seen him and Novarreno's attempt to blackmail him had cost him his life. But that he might be in the very same room...

"What are you trying to tell us, Engel?"

Engel had picked up the doll and was holding her upside down by the leg. Livening up, he replied, using the doll to gesticulate. His overcoat fell open, revealing the white pyjamas stretched tight across his body. He looked like a buffoon.

"The letters were written to terrify, and to render this tragedy easier to execute. Only one of us could know the story, and know where to have all the heirs meet. *And only one of us could have any interest in the deaths of the others.*"

"But why?" shouted Besesti.

Flemington got up and looked at Engel.

"What do you mean, Mr Engel?"

The pachyderm turned slowly to contemplate the lawyer. He sneered.

"No one could understand better than you, Flemington of Lincoln's Inn Fields, since you're a lawyer, what interest an heir might have *in being the only one left to receive the inheritance!*"

Besesti interrupted:

"In that case, I'm excluded from any suspicion. I expect nothing from Alton. And I'm waiting to hear why I've been made to join this hellish meeting."

The sane, quiet voice of Da Como was heard as he turned to the inspector.

"I don't have anything to do with it either. I'll be damned if I ever play another trick in my life—my having put the doll on Engel's bed was nothing but a joke. Why have you made me come down here?"

De Vincenzi suddenly started. The doll! The two dolls Mary Alton had gone to get! She had not come back!

"Sani!" shouted a lacerating voice.

"Here I am," Sani answered, rushing in from the lobby.

"Who is guarding the first floor?"

The deputy inspector paled. "No one—it's true! I was there but then I came down after that woman."

Pushing Sani aside, De Vincenzi rushed for the main staircase. But he hadn't even reached the first landing when he stopped. Mary Alton had appeared before him. She was descending slowly, the two dolls in her arms.

"Ah," the inspector sighed. Then he recovered himself and smiled. "I was afraid you weren't able to find Carin Nolan's doll."

"I had to look in all her drawers, as a matter of fact. I couldn't find it. It was in a hat box in the wardrobe."

"Good."

He let Mary go ahead of him and followed behind her, waiting for her to enter the blue room.

"Go up to the first floor and stand guard in the corridor. Rooms 7 and 19 are occupied, as you know. Take special care with Room 7, and if you hear the slightest suspicious noise, enter immediately."

"I'll make sure of it," Sani hurriedly reassured him, hoping to excuse his earlier forgetfulness.

"Are you armed?"

"Yes," and he showed De Vincenzi his revolver, which bulged in his jacket pocket.

De Vincenzi went back into the blue room. The widow had put one doll on the table and was sitting with the other in her arms, holding it tight against her breast. It was her doll. The one on the table, even though similar in all respects to the other two, had on a little blue silk dress. Why were the others, then, both dressed in pink gauze?

"Mr Engel, when your brother went back to Africa and you kept the doll with you, what was it wearing?"

"What are you talking about?" Engel asked, astonished. He couldn't understand how the doll's clothing mattered in such a tragedy.

It was Mrs Flemington who answered. "I sewed the two pink gauze dresses. My husband asked me to do it. Harry Alton had begged him to organize two dresses for the dolls."

"Harry was afraid that Lessinger would come to London, discover the dolls and recognize them as the ones that had belonged to his sisters. He wanted them destroyed, and he asked Engel and his wife for them. But both Engel and Mrs Mary refused to hand them over. So he thought their clothes should be changed. It was my wife, as she said, who made the dresses."

"What about this one?" the inspector asked, pointing to the blue doll.

"Carin Nolan was living in Norway. After the death of her grandfather, the doll was sent to Christiana from the Transvaal."

"But, Mrs Alton, didn't you tell your husband you'd lost it?"

"I don't remember," the widow replied. And she wrinkled her forehead. "The fact is, I had grown fond of the doll and wouldn't let Harry have it back, or maybe I asked him to let me have it. I don't remember. Maybe I said both those things. Harry was very suspicious, and not easy to deceive. But I don't see what importance—"

"In fact, it doesn't have any."

"It's definitely true about the clothes," Engel suddenly exclaimed. "One day, Harry came to me and he himself changed the dress in front of my very eyes. The blue dress was burnt in the fireplace in my room."

"Mr Flemington, read the will!"

Flemington stood up. He was clearly disturbed. He hesitated before walking to the black suitcase he'd left on the chair after putting it there in order to find the letter signed by Julius Lessinger.

"Inspector, you must take responsibility for reading the will at such a dangerous time."

"It's essential, Mr Flemington." De Vincenzi looked one by one at the people surrounding him. Anxious expectancy was written on each face—everyone's except for Besesti's. He'd collapsed after his confession, elbows on the table, head in his hands, looking down. He remained immobile.

Flemington opened the suitcase and took out a large black leather portfolio. He went back to the table and drew from that an oversized envelope bearing five red seals. On the reverse, one could see four or five lines of the heavy, deliberate handwriting De Vincenzi had already noticed on the letter written by the major to his wife.

Flemington sat down. He read from the envelope he was holding:

> *To be opened after my death in the presence of the three dolls and Douglas Layng, Carin Nolan, Vilfredo Engel, Pompeo Besesti, Mary Alton. The reading must take place in The Hotel of the Three Roses in Milan (Italy). It must be read personally by the lawyer George Flemington, who will be accompanied by his wife, Mrs Diana Flemington.*

The lawyer raised his head to look at his wife. Diana Flemington immediately stopped crying. Flemington's nervous fingers lifted the red seals, one after another.

"Do you have a knife?"

Da Como was the first to get up and hold out a long penknife, which he'd opened. He returned to his chair in the corner. Flemington glanced at the open door, then at the inspector. De Vincenzi got up and closed the door. The blade of the penknife cut through the envelope, and Flemington's fingers drew out a large sheet of paper folded in four. The reading of Harry Alton's will was brief.

> *I leave all I possess to the three dolls, once the property of Donald Lessinger's daughters. They alone are my legitimate heirs. The benefit of the goods which the dolls will thus possess shall be enjoyed by those to whom they have been entrusted. The doll temporarily given to my wife must be returned immediately to Douglas Layng after the reading of this will. Although the capital shall remain secure and inalienable, the usufruct shall be transferred from the three owners of the dolls to their own natural heirs until their extinction, at which time the life interest shall be enjoyed by the British Red Cross. This is my will, which my legal adviser and friend George Flemington will see carried out and respected. I, Harry Alton, being of sound mind and body, do hereby wish and decree.*
>
> *Sydney, November 1919*

A deathly silence followed the lawyer's words. Mary Alton stood up. She held the doll to her chest, her fingers wrapped tightly around it. Her pallor was waxen.

"What does it mean?"

Flemington turned to look at her.

"It means, Mrs Alton, that your husband is not leaving you a cent of his possessions."

"It's not possible! That is *not* my husband's will!" Her voice was cutting and the words forced through her teeth. Her whole body was shaking.

"What are you trying to imply?" Flemington asked.

De Vincenzi quietly watched Mary Alton. She had changed completely. Her violet eyes had turned into tiny, flashing emeralds. Her passionate, red-painted lips were now an open wound on a bloodless face.

"I deny that this is the will of my husband. There's been a substitution. I know the real will of Harry Alton."

Flemington put the large document on the table in front of him. "It's true," he said slowly. "Major Alton did draw up another will before this one, and he entrusted it to me. But the authenticity of the present will cannot be doubted, and since it is dated later, the previous one is annulled."

Mary Alton was quivering. But she sensed the inspector's eyes on her and kept quiet. Her features softened, and she recovered her air of inscrutable innocence.

"What was the date of the preceding will?" asked De Vincenzi.

"It was drawn up on the same day as the wedding in this hotel. The witnesses were me and an English doctor who was passing through Milan and whom the pastor had asked to attend Alton's wedding."

"Do you remember the terms of that will, Mr Flemington?"

"You see!" the widow interrupted again. "The second will is invalid. It doesn't bear the witnesses' signatures."

"You're mistaken, Mrs Mary. You're mistaken!"

208

The lawyer showed her the document, pointing out the signatures of two other people following the major's.

"There are the witnesses' signatures. There's also a codicil." He read:

> *This will annuls any preceding will and constitutes the "surprise" I announced to my wife.*

"Do you remember the instructions of the previous will?" De Vincenzi repeated.

"That one divided the inheritance four ways: three parts went to Vilfredo Engel, Douglas Layng and Carin Nolan. The fourth was destined for Mary Vendramini. In case of the death of one of the heirs, the survivors inherited the part of the deceased."

He watched the widow approach the table, put down the doll she'd been clasping in her arms till then, and slowly retreat. She continued to look as cool as a cucumber, and her extreme pallor, heightened by the harsh light of the lamp, was frightening. Everyone stared at her. She moved like a zombie.

"Mrs Alton!" ordered the inspector.

"My presence is no longer necessary now I know what the surprise is."

"You're forgetting that there are two bodies you must step over in order to leave here."

She raised her head and turned on them a look strangely rapt and luminous. "What do they have to do with me? *It's the dolls who inherit!*"

For the first time she laughed: a low, broken, inhuman laugh. Chilling. It was impossible to believe she was the one laughing, so still had she remained, her look so pure and innocent.

A piercing scream rang out. "Murderer! You are the murderer of my son!"

Diana Flemington leapt from the sofa and started for Mary. Her husband was the first to stop her, seizing her in his arms. He took her away, still squeezing her against his chest and holding her head against his own shoulder with a tenderness that was new and surprising for such a large, gruff and sarcastic man.

Mary Alton heard the scream but didn't even draw back. She gave a faint shrug and shook her head at the tirade. She looked at the inspector and said with deep pity, "Poor Mrs Flemington." By now she'd completely recovered her remarkable equilibrium, and was calm and assured. Her eyes were no longer shining; they'd returned to their deep, dark violet colour. The accusation had not hit home, and she appeared to find it too absurd to consider.

"What do you intend to do *now*, Signora Alton?"

De Vincenzi spoke to her in Italian because he wanted to spare Diana Flemington the torment that would result in her hearing everything Mary was about to say.

"Get away from here! There's nothing more to keep me in this place."

"Yes, some*thing* and some*one can* keep you here! Your accomplice, for example."

Mary stared at him. One might have said she looked amused. "I don't understand!"

"Wait a moment and you will." He walked past her into the lobby. He signalled to the two officers to stand guard by the blue room: "*No one* must leave! Keep them from leaving here, even if you have to shoot." He then hurried up the main stairs and ran into Sani at the start of the corridor. "Did you hear any movement?" He pointed to Room 7.

210

"No. Nothing. I even put my ear to the door, but couldn't hear a breath."

"What?" This time the shout was De Vincenzi's. He grabbed the handle and flung open the door. He uttered a curse, a terrible curse against himself. How had he not foreseen this? There, on the floor beside the bed, lay Al Righetti. He'd been shot as he got out of bed, since he'd pulled the sheets and the bedcover along with him when he fell. He was bent over, with his forehead against the bedside rug and his arms flung open.

De Vincenzi leant over to lift him up and laid him on the bed with Sani's help.

"He's dead," said Sani.

A spot of blood on his breast had stained his light-coloured pyjamas purple. Another spot could be seen on the rug, darker and thicker. He hadn't bled much.

"But he was shot with a revolver, this one!" Sani exclaimed in terrified surprise. "Almost point-blank."

Indeed, his silk jacket was haloed with burn marks from a shot just out of the barrel. The revolver lay on the floor—they saw it only now. A small revolver with an ivory grip. De Vincenzi bent to pick it up, and Sani made a move to deter him.

"The fingerprints!"

"There aren't any," the inspector muttered. "There can't be any." He picked up a little yellow satin cushion lying nearby. "See? She had the revolver hidden inside this cushion. She came up to Al Righetti, who wouldn't have suspected her and probably wanted to embrace her, and she pressed the cushion to his chest as she fired. That's why no one heard the shot." He indicated burn marks on the satin identical to the ones on the pyjamas.

"Her?" Sani's eyes widened. "But whom do you mean?"

"Yes. It was the only way for her to have the entire inheritance and to prevent her accomplice from speaking."

He was scowling, his jaws clenched, his lips pursed. He studied the body: the wide-open eyes expressed nothing but enormous shock.

"Go and get Bardi and bring him back here."

Sani had given up asking for explanations. He left.

Alone again, De Vincenzi studied the room. He was gripped by feverish excitement. *He knew the whole story now!* The spark that had been missing for so long had lit up his brain. A horrific drama… He ran straight from the bed to the window. The shutters had been thrown back and the first light of day was coming through, dulled by the rain. He began examining the windowsill, knelt down on the floor. His intuition had been right. He could see that the edges of the wooden windowsill and the floor tiles were still damp, and someone had tried to dry them. In order to kill Novarreno, Al Righetti had gone out of his window and come in through the Levantine's window. The simplest gymnastic feat. He hadn't needed the stairs to get down to the courtyard or climb out of it, not at all! He'd held on to the cornice that circled the building, continuing the line of the windowsills along the wall.

De Vincenzi turned back to the bed. In a corner between the wall and the wardrobe he spotted a small oil stove. It would have served to overheat the air in Douglas Layng's room so that his body hadn't gone rigid. The one he had been looking for…

He'd guessed it all, he had, in every detail. The only thing was, he hadn't managed to see it all at once. But how could he? How could he have known that Julius Lessinger was dead? His very name on each person's tongue; that ghostly avenger whom everyone named as if fearing he were behind them. The actual existence of Julius Lessinger, *in whom he'd had to believe*, had derailed him, forcing him to look in every other direction. It was true that he'd suspected Nicola Al Righetti, and for that very reason he hadn't wished to question him further, or enter his room. After Carin Nolan had been injured it didn't seem possible that the man could attempt any other crimes, and he hadn't wanted to put him under suspicion before he had the evidence.

But how could he have guessed that *she* would kill him? Yet now he would have said that her killing him was unavoidable. Mary Alton absolutely had to prevent her first husband from speaking. A nagging sense of unease or remorse plagued him. *He had sent her alone to get the dolls, precisely because he wanted her to betray herself.* Yes, when it came down to it, Al Righetti's death was his fault. And when he'd run to the first floor and met her on the staircase with the two dolls in her arms, she'd seemed so calm, so completely innocent—and beautiful—that he'd reproached himself for having set her up and told himself again that he was on the wrong track.

He continued searching the room. He opened the wardrobe and saw a silk shirt on a hanger. He looked at the sleeves. A bit of broken stitching hung from the buttonhole of one of the cuffs—and there was the golden disc with its three blue and red enamel circles; the other disc—the one he'd found in the built-in wardrobe on the third floor—was in his pocket. He closed the wardrobe and looked in the dresser drawers, then in the table drawer. Nothing. There were linens, clothes, boxes for collars and ties. Hidden under the shirts in the first drawer was a big Colt, black and sinister, with a silencer on the barrel: an American gangster's weapon. But no letter, no papers. He continued looking, increasingly agitated. What he hoped to find, even he could not say.

He noticed a suitcase and went over to open it. His movements had become clumsy. Only his nervous excitement kept him from wilting, from keeling over after that diabolical night. He'd come to the hotel at ten last night and now it was almost eight in the morning—ten hours. He was afraid of totting up the hours, of imagining that *something worse* might lie in store for him…

He kept seeing that pure, oval face before him, white as wax and framed by a mass of shining golden hair… two deep, violet-coloured eyes… a simple, graceful, fragile body. He emptied the suitcase onto the floor. Ties, linens, some men's jewellery. Another, smaller revolver. So, nothing. But what was he hoping to find?

Finally he found it. A few yellowed pages, some of them torn and some covered with directions and names written in pen. Just what he'd dimly guessed as soon as the old Bernasconi had told him about the young man who always met Mary Vendramini in Milan. Nicola Al Righetti had secretly married Mary Vendramini in Chicago in 1911, and those yellowed sheets were the documents that certified their marriage.

By now, it was all clear. Realizing how rich Major Alton was, Mary hadn't hesitated to contract a second marriage—in agreement with her first husband—in order to get her hands on the money, and to inherit it when the time came. The time had come. De Vincenzi jumped as if someone had whipped him—he felt a sigh, a sort of wheezing, behind him. He put the papers in his pocket and turned round.

The hunchback was standing at the door, looking at the dead man on the bed, his eyes wide with fear.

De Vincenzi got up. "Signor Bardi, do you recognize this man?"

He looked at him.

"What? What do you mean?"

"This man was in this hotel in 1914. Do you recognize him?"

The hunchback had a brainwave. It was just as if his pale, yellow, angular face had suddenly lit up.

"Yes," he shouted. "Yes! That's it! He's the man who was with Mary Vendramini."

"Fine. That's all." De Vincenzi signalled to Sani to take him away. "Make sure he does not leave his room."

"Who killed him?" asked Bardi in his strident but firm voice.

"It doesn't matter right now. You'll find out. Go." And he followed the two, closing the door behind him and starting down the stairs. *Oh to be done with this, and to be done with it as soon as possible.* What was waiting for him down below in the blue room?

The two officers stood at the door.

"Nothing?"

They shook their heads and moved aside. Inside, everyone was as he had left them. The widow, who turned to watch him, was also still waiting.

"Mrs Mary Alton, you are under arrest for the murder of Nicola Al Righetti, your first and only husband since the second marriage you contracted with Major Alton is null and void; and for complicity in the murders of Douglas Layng and Giorgio Novarreno, and for wounding Carin Nolan."

The woman continued staring at him. After their initial shock, the others around her—George and Diana Flemington, Vilfredo Engel, Carlo Da Como and Pompeo Besesti—sat in suspended silence, as if pinned to the floor by a new anxiety, by the sensation that something awful, unexpected, even fatal was about to happen.

215

De Vincenzi repeated the charge. Mary Alton moved towards the table, picked up the two dolls, clasped them to her breast, kissed them and then sat down, where she began gently cradling them, caressing them and speaking to them in her measured voice, as harmonious as music, as sweet and nostalgic as a love song.

"You're mine… mine, both of you… I'll keep you for ever with me… good sisters… With me for ever!"

They took her in the car, through the rain, through streets and avenues and over fields, with the two porcelain dolls. They went through a gate, and then the car stopped in front of a large white building surrounded by flower beds. Two men in dark-blue shirts came to take her from Deputy Inspector Sani. Shortly afterwards a gentleman with a large, aquiline nose and gold-framed glasses received her in a dazzling, all-white room, where he began to observe her with intense curiosity. And all the while she cradled her dolls, singing lullabies of innocence.

20

After speaking to the investigating magistrate and dictating the longest passages of his report, Inspector De Vincenzi went off with his two officers, leaving only one of them at The Hotel of the Three Roses to guard Rooms 5, 6, 7 and 9, which the magistrate had locked and sealed. Another stretcher had already carried away the body of Nicola Al Righetti.

In the lobby, Da Como and Engel were sitting quietly on the sofa. Some way away Pompeo Besesti was stretched out on a chair, staring into space. Engel was still wearing his white pyjamas under his overcoat. It was ten in the morning, and the rain continued to fall. From the window a parade of open umbrellas could be seen on the pavement.

"I don't understand," the harsh, deep voice came suddenly, "how the American kept Layng's body hidden until that evening."

"The inspector understood it," Da Como replied. He'd been present when De Vincenzi had dictated his report and had his meetings with the magistrate. "The young man was killed at midday when he went up to his room after he returned from a walk. After stabbing him to death, the American feared that the blood would leave visible traces in the room, so he covered the body with sheets."

"But why was Layng in his pyjamas? And why had he gone to bed?"

"He wasn't feeling well. Maybe they made him drink something. He'd told Stella Essington that he wasn't feeling well, and at eight that evening she came to his room and saw both the body and the killer. When she heard that Al Righetti was dead, she talked. The body stayed in Room 5 for the whole day, and the American locked the door."

"But to get it upstairs?"

"He seized on the moment when everyone was downstairs in the dining room. Al Righetti ate, as usual, in the billiard room. Pietro served him, but of course Al Righetti was often on his own in there. So it was easy for him to go up the service stairway, which communicates directly with the corridor on the first floor. Only Bardi posed any danger to him, and only for an instant. But the American made it in time and took advantage of the moment of panic to go back down to the billiard room without being seen, and then to rush from there to the dining room."

Silence. Then again, that deep, hoarse voice: "But how did they think they could get away with it?"

"She was the instigator—the woman. She knew the story of Julius Lessinger from Alton and she continued to keep the major's fear alive, hoping to make use of the story with Al Righetti's help. They didn't want to kill him and they couldn't, because Mary had read the first will which the major made when he married her. She wanted to inherit the whole of it. When Alton wrote to tell her he was about to die, and Flemington then informed her of the meeting to be held in this hotel, she wrote the letter from Hamburg and conceived of the whole diabolical scheme."

"What about me?" asked the deep, hoarse voice, broken by a hiccup.

"For you, old friend, they had in store an 'accidental' death caused by the sight of the man hanging on the landing. You can thank Bardi—he saved your life."

Engel laughed in his thundering way, which caused Besesti to leap from his armchair. "I wouldn't have died! I'm thick-skinned."

Da Como firmly agreed.

A further silence followed. Virgilio crossed the lobby from the direction of the staircase. He was looser and more disjointed than ever, his legs going haywire and his arms in front of him, as if he were afraid of falling. He walked over to the desk and stopped. His wife, placid, white and matronly, was still drawing circles with her pencil on the back of that day's menu. Mario went behind the bar.

"Mario, bring me an *aperitivo*," ordered Da Como.

The four *scopone* players went back to their corner table in the dining room and started up their interminable games once more. They'd removed their collars and ties, their faces were exhausted and their eyes ringed with dark circles. They smoked and drank without let-up.

"I cannot understand how the sevens can be broken up in the first hand," Verdulli squawked.

Da Como was just bringing the glass of liquor to his mouth when his hand stopped in mid-air. He stared at the door.

Three women had appeared in the entrance, one after the other. Each wore ribbons—claret, mauve or black—on an austere dress, and their profiles were exactly the same: beak-like under sequinned hats.

Da Como stood up and moved towards them cheerfully.

"What's new, dear sisters?"

Claret Ribbons spoke. "Jolanda wanted to come back here."

Mauve Ribbons pursed her lips in disgust.

Black Ribbons whined, "We'll give you ten thousand."

"Eight thousand!" the eldest snapped.

"Ten thousand," Jolanda pleaded.

Just then, while Carlo Da Como smiled sarcastically, preparing his response, the telephone rang. Mario ran to answer it and immediately reappeared at the door to the toilets—for the phone was in there—holding the receiver in one hand.

"Signor Besesti, the Bank of Pure Metals is on the line…"

Did you know?

In 1929, when the Italian publisher Mondadori launched their popular series of crime and thriller titles (clad in the yellow jackets that would later give their name to the wider *giallo* tradition of Italian books and films) there were no Italian authors on the list. Many thought that Italy was inherently infertile ground for the thriller genre, with one critic claiming that a detective novel set in such a sleepy Mediterranean country was an "absurd hypothesis". Augusto De Angelis strongly disagreed. He saw crime fiction as the natural product of his fraught and violent times: "The detective novel is the fruit – the red, bloodied fruit of our age."

The question had a political significance too – the Marxist Antonio Gramsci was fascinated by the phenomenon of crime fiction, and saw in its unifying popularity a potential catalyst for revolutionary change. Benito Mussolini and his Fascist regime were also interested in the genre, although their attitude towards it was confused – on the one hand they approved of the triumph of the forces of order over degeneracy and chaos that most thriller plots involved; on the other hand they were wary of representations of their Italian homeland as anything less than a harmonious idyll.

This is the background against which Augusto De Angelis's *The Murdered Banker* appeared in 1935, the first of 20 novels starring Inspector De Vincenzi to be published over the next eight years. This period saw the peak of the British Golden Age puzzle mystery tradition, and the rise of the American hardboiled genre. However, De Angelis created a style all his own, with a detective who is more complex than the British "thinking machine" typified by Sherlock Holmes, but more sensitive than the tough-guy American private eye.

His originality won De Angelis great popularity, and a reputation as the father of the Italian mystery novel. Unfortunately, it also attracted the attention of the Fascist authorities, who censored De Angelis's work. After writing a number of anti-Fascist articles, De Angelis was finally arrested in 1943. Although he was released three months later, he was soon beaten up by a Fascist thug and died from his injuries in 1944.

So, where do you go from here?

To follow De Vincenzi on his next investigation, as he hunts a killer among the mannequins of a Milan fashion house, pick up *The Mystery of the Three Orchids*.

Or, if you fancy attempting to solve a seemingly impossible series of crimes, take a look at Soji Shimada's legendary locked-room mystery, *The Tokyo Zodiac Murders*.

AVAILABLE AND COMING SOON
FROM PUSHKIN VERTIGO

Jonathan Ames

You Were Never Really Here

Augusto De Angelis

The Murdered Banker
The Mystery of the Three Orchids
The Hotel of the Three Roses

María Angélica Bosco

Death Going Down

Piero Chiara

The Disappearance of Signora Giulia

Frédéric Dard

The Switch
The Wretches
The Wicked Go to Hell

Martin Holmén

Clinch

Alexander Lernet-Holenia

I Was Jack Mortimer

Boileau-Narcejac

Vertigo
She Who Was No More

Leo Perutz

Master of the Day of Judgment
Little Apple
St Peter's Snow

Soji Shimada

The Tokyo Zodiac Murders

Seishi Yokomizo

The Inugami Clan